Memoirs of the Legendary
Cannabis Cowboy

ॐ

Robert G Schmidt

Published by Medical Marijuana of America
www.MedicalMarijuanaOfAmerica.com

ISBN 978-0-615-26251-2

*This book is dedicated to
Rhonda Helane Numark as without her
Faith in me and the Unconditional Love
she has blessed me with, I would not be
here to have written it.*

Contents

Introduction by Tim Castleman... 1
1967, Draft Evaders on the Katie L.. 7
August 1969 – Woodstock 13
1970 Bowling Green & Kent State... 19
A2 23
June, 1975 – RED CLOUD 29
July, 1975 – Crash & Burn.. 33
September, 1975 – Cartagena.. 37
October, 1975: The JOE LOUIS 41
1976 – The Aquarian Sea 53
Portland, Maine 63
1978 - The DAKOTA DC3 67
1978 - The POLAR SEA.. 73
November, 1978 - Orange Sunrise 77
The Miyako Hotel.. 81
Dan's Overdose 89
Ray's Death 95
My Arrest... 99
The Deal 105
Rhonda... 111
Summer 1996, Petaluma.. 119
Establishing Ties in Mendocino 123
The Democratic Convention, San Jose, 2000... 127
Santa Cruz 133
The VAN Hotel 135
Patients, Pills, People 137
Home Invasion... 143
The Debate... 147
The New Offices and the Circle Star Ranch 153
The DEA Raid on the Genesis 1:29 Ranch 165
Incarceration 2006-2008... 171
Epilogue... 175

Introduction by Tim Castleman

Early summer of 2001 I took a trip up Hwy 101 to view marijuana gardens with my new friend, Duke, otherwise known as "The Legendary Cannabis Cowboy", founder and head proprietor of Genesis 1:29, A Compassionate Foundation.

The plants behind this 4 ft x 8 ft "Genesis 1:29" sign were cannabis.

I had met Duke earlier in the year at the Santa Cruz Industrial Hemp Expo – he had come up with some very high-grade herb and gave me his business card, inviting me to visit his dispensary anytime.

This trip was an introduction to large-scale cannabis production. The truck, one of several he was making payments on to Ford Motor Company through the local dealer, was an F250 4 door Diesel pickup. It had been lifted and modified to accommodate huge knobby tires that rubbed the wheel wells when turning too sharp, and made a noise like a dive-bomber screaming up the highway. Duke really liked this effect, as he was sort of enamored with the whole WW2 thing.

With us were his two dogs, Dakota (a big black Australian Shepherd) and Moonie (a large rottweiler). They occupied the back seat and took turns trying to occupy the seat I was using. These dogs meant the world to Duke, and they went everywhere with him. They were very obedient and well trained to do just what he asked them – and he was pretty well trained to accommodate their every need.

Also on board was a tin of marijuana buds. These were not your ordinary nuggets. These buds were six to eight inches long, and a couple of inches around. This was the finest weed in the world, homegrown northern California skunk. He had a glass pipe that he cleaned every morning before leaving the house and wore a windproof lighter on a string around his neck. Duke does not use tobacco, so the lighter was strictly for smoking cannabis.

When he smoked, he would break off a thumb-sized piece of bud and jam it into the bowl. Most of the time he would then just light up – but sometimes, if we were at the office, he would then dribble some of his honey oil on it first. Honey oil is a concentrate of the active ingredients in marijuana extracted with laboratory grade ethanol and a vacuum separator.

We never used the oil on any of these road trips as it would have been way too much trouble in a moving vehicle, and speed limits were something Duke seemed completely oblivious to. So off we roared, dogs, herb, me and Duke in his 4 door Diesel truck that would easily squish smaller cars with little more than a "bump-in-the-road" effect, due to its massive size. Our destination was unknown to me at this point; I only knew we were going for a ride "up north to see the marijuana gardens."

Driving somewhere, anywhere, with Duke is a real adventure. First of all there are these two large dogs drooling all over the place. And they are his babies, especially the black lab, Dakota. Whenever we stopped somewhere, if I got out of my seat, Dakota would promptly claim it as hers. If Dakota somehow missed the opportunity, Moonie would quickly fill it. Upon my return it would take a great deal of coaxing to get them into the back seat and re-claim my spot.

Another aspect of the adventure is the completely open use of marijuana. There never was ANY attempt to conceal it in any way. Duke would prove to be the most brazen pot smoker I have met.

Well, as I said, off we roared at 80 MPH up Highway 101, with Duke talking almost non-stop, telling me stories of his days as a tug boat captain, pot smuggler and iron worker. He did spin some incredible stories of his adventures in South America as a pot smuggler, and of his family's ownership of a Great Lakes boat company of some sort. According to Duke, the family controlled all of the shipping in the Great Lakes Region. However, somehow, it just seemed hard to believe. I didn't really know, one way or the other, so I decided to just give this larger-than- life character all the room he needed to be who he wanted to be.

After a few hours we turned off the 101 and drove into the wilderness. It was a great comfort to drive through miles and miles of forest, with many areas still unspoiled by the power grid and the teeming masses. Yes, the scars on mountain sides are all too visible, remnants of clear cutting operations, but there was lots of new growth sprouting up, and on a sunny summer evening from the cab of the monster air conditioned diesel truck it looked postcard-pretty. The roar of the huge knobby tires bothered me but Duke loved it and wanted the biggest, meanest tires he could find. As I would learn later on the side of a mountain in Siskiyou County, even these 35 inch tall monster truck tires were not aggressive enough for Duke.

We drove down a dirt road for a couple of miles and then we came upon our site: a manufactured house and a chain link fence surrounding a field of approximately 1200 nearly mature marijuana plants. The field sloped facing southeast and at the foot of the slope were a cargo container and travel trailer, the curing/trim room and caretaker's residence. On the gate there was a wooden plaque inscribed with references to California Statute 11362.5 & 11362.9 and also the name of the dispensary. (Duke was a real stickler for people to quit using the term "Prop 215" in favor of quoting the actual law that resulted from the "Proposition", I have to admit I see his point and so have adopted the practice myself.)

In the middle of the field was a giant red cross, like the ones used on M.A.S.H. to alert the enemy flying overhead of the compassionate nature of the operation. One of the caretakers came running to the gate, overjoyed to see Duke, and his dogs, and the load of supplies we had brought them.

This remote field of marijuana reminded me of a M.A.S.H. unit

Our next stop was in Siskiyou at Stan's place. (This field was raided a couple weeks after this visit, and for some reason the raiders left a substantial part of the crop harvested and stacked in a barn on the property overnight. Duke roared up highway 101 towing a super deluxe horse trailer and retrieved a substantial part of the crop.) I only had a cheap point and shoot camera to take a few pictures – notice the paper tags stapled to the stalks, these were on the plants when we unloaded the horse trailer, supposedly put there by law enforcement agents.

By now the sun was down and it was getting cold. We still had another stop to make so despite plea's to stay the night, we had a quick bowl of soup and were back on 101 roaring our way to the next stop, the ranch and grow operation of Duke's "Brother" Franklin.

We arrived at Frank's very late in the night. There was some tension related to his wife, who I never met. We did go inside his house, which was under construction with a large room set aside for an indoor grow setup. Another grower also lived on the property in another house, and we all gathered for a late night smokeout inside the room under construction. A smokeout would involve packing bowls full of quality herb, dripping honey oil on some, and sampling several varieties and flavors. It was impossible to keep track of it all, and I didn't bother trying.

Robert G. Schmidt in Siskiyou County

During the smokeout I stepped outside and looked around a bit. I saw several pieces of specialty type equipment – a Yamaha 4 wheel drive trail truck, a tractor, and lots of general garden tools. Yep, these guys were serious about growing marijuana!

Over the next year I visited a few more times and watched Duke's Genesis 1:29 grow and evolve until September 2002 when federal D.E.A. agents conducted raids on his ranch and dispensary, seizing over 3000 plants. After a lengthy legal process, Duke made a deal and had to serve time in federal prison. Following is his story, in his own words, written while he was in prison.

Cannabis Cowboy

1967, Draft Evaders on the Katie L.

Growing up on an island in Lake Erie (Put-in-Bay, Ohio) provided an environment to be a 'natural' boat runner. I had a skiff before I had a bicycle. Boats were more of a necessity than cars, as the island was only about three miles long by two miles wide, and only had seventeen miles of paved road.

The community included three islands, North Bass, Middle Bass and South Bass. Like a time capsule, it had not evolved much since its grand days during Prohibition, when bootlegging and whisky smuggling created the financial cornerstones of the current businesses and tourism trade.

There were nine wineries and thirty-one bars on Middle Bass and South Bass; Put-in-Bay was the Port of Call the ferries used as the primary destination for tourists from the mainland. Put-in-Bay was the hub, and that is where I lived.

The old guys always talked about the "good ole' days" during Prohibition. As a child I could never hear enough about their adventures. I would remember and savor every detail about pick-up points, passages through the reefs and secret coves that most islanders did not know about. It was like learning the holy grail of a secret society that only had a few select members. I learned the unwritten history about the island many knew, but few talked about.

These old rumrunners taught me everything there was to know about taking care of your boat. When to make a run and how to be invisible. Loose lips sink ships. Watch your fuel. Don't run hard unless you are chased. Keep your boat seaworthy with the fuel tanks topped off at all times, she is the only thing between you and a watery grave. The most important rule was: A master boat operator uses his wisdom and insight to keep him out of situations that would require his expert abilities. Last but not least, were the five P's – Prior Planning Prevents Poor Performance. Even with all of this in hand and faithfully practiced, Murphy's Law could change everything in a flash.

My father chartered and restored classic speedboats. On Sunday evenings when things quieted down, we would refuel and wash them down so that they were ready to go the next day. Most of these boats were built by the masters in the 1920's, and had been used for whisky running out of Canada. They were sleek, fast and beautiful pieces of art, composed of mahogany and oak construction highlighted with plated fittings and leather upholstery. The only changes made during restoration were the installation of modern engines, as the originals were no longer manufactured. These old rumrunners had charm and design that were unique to this area, and they served us well. The tourists loved to be taken for rides, and chartered them to get from one island to another.

The Vietnam War was all the news of the day and many of my friends were either in the Army or the Marines. I was 16 and my older brother was in a place called the Mekong Delta running a PBR (Patrol Boat River).

Earlier that summer I had met two people from Ann Arbor, Michigan. Pete and Kate were "hippies" so to speak, and were visiting the island on Memorial weekend. We had never seen flower children before and only knew about them from the newspapers, radio and TV. I knew they opposed the war in Vietnam and I agreed with that philosophy. We became fast friends, and I introduced them to the locals.

After the weekend festivities came to an end my new friends decided to stay a couple more days to fully grasp the "island experience" without the drunken

The Katie L. was a classic wood speedboat photo by Roy Hulsbergen – Bigstockphoto.com

tourists crowding everything. My friends and I showed up at their campsite in the State Park to barbeque chicken and drink beer. We were listening to 8-track tapes of Bob Dylan, Simon and Garfunkel, the Byrds, the Mommas and the Pappas and smoking hashish. Soon the conversation turned to the war. They told me that some people were leaving for Canada to avoid the draft. This sounded logical to me and I wanted to help.

Then the light bulb went on in my head. If my family had smuggled whisky out of Canada in speedboats, then why couldn't I smuggle draft dodgers into Canada? It would be much easier than whisky running. It had moral fiber. Most of all, it was an exciting idea.

The next evening I took Pete and Kate on a boat ride and proceeded to make plans, and work out all of the details. The round trip from the State Park on South Bass Island to Point Pelee State Park in Canada was approximately 70 miles. I thought I could make the round trip in less than three hours under any weather conditions. On Friday those who needed this service would come to the island by ferryboat, and camp at the State Park for the weekend. On Sunday evening I would sneak the Katie L. out of the marina at midnight, and run around the west shore of the island to pick up my waiting passengers at the State Park. We would then make the 35 mile run to Point Pelee State Park in Ontario, where there would be people waiting to pick them up. I would then run back to the island, put the Katie L. back in her slip and be home in bed by 3 AM – no one would be the wiser. Or so I thought. The inaugural run would prove to be much more complicated.

On Sunday night of the 4th of July weekend things were pretty quiet when I headed down to the marina at about 11:30. I noticed the wind was up out of the northeast. This has always been a sign of some treacherous weather, but I had a schedule to keep. I checked the oil and fuel of the Katie L. and put the *tonneau* cover over the aft cockpit to keep out the spray, and in case it rained.

I backed her out of the slip and headed out of the harbor. The waves were about three feet tall and spaced close together. "This is not going to be a comfortable ride," I thought. In fact, we are going to be fighting an uphill battle all of the way to Point Pelee. I was lucky that the Katie L.'s builders knew when they designed and constructed her that she would be required to provide service in these conditions. This was actually excellent smuggling weather. No one in their right mind would be out in these conditions.

On the run to the State Park at Put-in-Bay I had to follow the west shore of the island, which was a pleasant ride. I was starting to believe the trip would not be as bad as I expected when I pulled up to the dock. There were four passengers bound for Canada, but two had brought their girlfriends and a lot of baggage.

The Katie L. had seating for nine so we piled the luggage in the rear cockpit and covered it; then four people sat in the center, two sat with me in the front and we were off.

Soon we passed Rattlesnake Island and, no longer in the lee of the islands, the wrath of the North Easter was upon us. The waves had grown to about five feet, and the wind was blowing thirty five to forty miles per hour. I adjusted my speed and course to head into the waves at a forty-five degree angle. I was running as fast as I dared to avoid pounding her hull, after all she was over 45 years old. It soon became clear this trip would take longer than expected.

We finally got to Point Pelee about 2:30 AM to find some anxious people waiting for us. We quickly unloaded the boat and smoked a couple bowls of hash as I said my goodbyes, because I was running late, and I had to get the Katie L. back before anyone found her missing. Shaking hands with one of the waiting men I was given a quarter pound of primo hash to take back with me. This was the finest kind, and was their way of expressing gratitude for services rendered. At this time in my life it was the foremost expression of gratitude I had yet experienced.

The ride back to Put-in-Bay would be better, as the boat was light, and running with the weather would allow me to surf the waves at a much faster speed. It all seemed too good to be true, but then a searchlight from a Canadian Coast Guard patrol boat struck me as I was leaving the park. This was very bad as I had the hash in my pocket and did not have permission to use the Katie L. Nor had I cleared customs or notified anyone of my voyage.

So I nailed it! I headed out into the night at full throttle – too scared to look back. It was like the spirit of the Katie L. was again alive. My heart was pounding and when she buried her nose into the bottom of a swell the spray stung my face and drenched me. I was cold and wet and high on hashish and adrenalin. I could feel the adventure that my uncles had felt when they were outrunning the Coast Guard during Prohibition. I was imagining that I was back in the day with a load of whisky. In fact I was smuggling, I did have a pocketful of hashish. I was outrunning a gunboat, and I was doing it in an old rumrunner. It was like the Katie L. and I were joined at the hip, her feel at the wheel, the hum of her engines, and her glide through the water were a synchronous harmony of speed and endurance. She was a thoroughbred from an era long gone by, and I was living the last of any quality experiences she had been designed for. Some may say I'm a romantic, but I feel I was blessed to pilot the last run of contraband on the Katie L. and I cherish the experience to this day.

I pulled into the harbor at Put-in-Bay around 4 AM and quietly docked the Katie L. back into her slip. I wiped her down and started up the hill when the headlights from my grandmother's Lincoln came on. Blinded by the lights I heard the door open. She spoke out, telling me to get in the car. "Where have you been? Do you know how much trouble you are in? Did you know the Canadian and U.S. Coast Guard are looking for the Katie L.?"

My grandfather, "Pop," had heard storm warnings on the air, and had gone to the marina to check on the boats. In an instant he had found the slip empty where the Katie L. should have been tied up. He notified the Coast Guard on both sides of the border. My family had assisted in many search and rescue missions over the decades. They knew Lake Erie well, and both Coast Guards knew my family well. A mutual respect and admiration had developed between us, as many lost boats were found and drowning victims recovered. The Great Lakes could be merciless at times, such as in the case of the Edmund Fitzgerald in 1975. Many times we were there to assist any way could.

I have never lied to my grandmother and I had to come clean. Reluctantly I told her about my underground railroad for draft evaders. To my surprise she was sympathetic, and advised me to keep my mouth shut and took me home to get some sleep.

The next morning the Canadian and U.S. Coast Guard forty footers were at the marina talking to my grandfather about the mysterious reappearance of the Katie L. She was in good shape with no apparent damage and no clues. Investigation over. Though there was one other detail from the Canadians. They claimed to have seen a boat that looked similar to the Katie L. the night before coming out of Point Pelee State Park. They lost sight of her as she took off into the darkness, outrunning them in the heavy seas. However, the weather conditions were too adverse to positively identify her as the Katie L. and I was never questioned by anyone - not even by my father, or Pop. It seems that my grandmother had drawn the line on this subject, though I could tell by my Mom's looks that she knew. On my birthday my grandmother gave me my own key to the Katie L. She said that she did not like me jumping the ignition, as it was a fire hazard.

After this I continued to run draft evaders into Canada through the summer of 1970. I think my grandmother enjoyed the continuation of a family tradition, though not a word was ever spoken about it.

August 1969 – Woodstock

It was a humid August afternoon, and most of my fellow Islanders and race participants were recuperating from the Inter Lake Yachting Association (I.L.Y.A.) Regatta Festival and Awards Banquet. This was an annual event in late July and early August, where the I.L.Y.A. would hold two weeks of sailing competition. There were several classes of sailboats that ranged from 18 feet to cruising boats in excess of 40 feet. It was two weeks of non-stop racing and drinking.

Robert G. Schmidt – Pre- Woodstock

I was pretty much burned out from sailing all day and partying all night. It was a relief to just kick-back with a joint and enjoy the peaceable atmosphere of island life. A sort of calm that follows a storm, a time to regenerate as Labor Day was soon approaching, and the insanity of another wave of tourists would flood paradise. The irony of all of this is that while many came to the island for its tranquility and old school charm, the mere presence of all these people eliminated the possibility of experiencing what they came for in the first place.

It was at this time that I noticed a familiar VW camper getting off of the ferryboat. It was Pete & Kate. I noticed that while they were driving towards us, sitting in the park, that a converted bread truck followed them. It was painted psychedelic with a large peace sign on each side.

They all pulled over by the cannons in the park. These cannons were from the British ships that were defeated by Oliver Hazard Perry in the

Lake Erie War of 1812. The park was one of the memorial sites that attracted tourists.

It was good to see them again, but I was curious about the timing. I thought that it may have been necessary to get the Katie L. ready for a run. That was not to be the case, though. They were just visiting with some of their friends for a couple of days before they headed for a rock concert in New York on the 15th, until the 17th. I had no idea what a rock concert was and their friends found that to be very humorous. They inquired as to whether I had ever been anywhere but the islands, and I said that I surely had. I claimed to have been to Detroit, Toledo, Port Clinton, Toronto, Cleveland, etc. It did not take them long to figure out that while in fact I had been to those cities that I had never gotten more than a hundred feet from the boat that took me there. Yes, I was at those places but only in the harbor to pick up cargo or passengers. I had never even seen a traffic light or bus.

It was then suggested that I go with them to Woodstock, New York, for three days of music - and to see what else was in the world. They expected at least 15,000 people there, and I was really excited at the concept of that many anti-war advocates at the same place, in the same time, for the same reason.

Over the next few days more of their friends arrived at Put in Bay to camp out until we would leave. There were about 30 of us, and I was really happy that all of them enjoyed the serene charm of the island. For most of them it was their first visit even though they had heard of the place before. As it turned out, some eventually bought property and moved to the island to start families. Some of them are still there to this day, as it is a unique and safe community of old school values for children to grow up in.

Then the morning arrived when we all packed up and boarded the ferries to go to the mainland and start this journey. To them it was a road trip, but to me it was an adventure. I was so excited that I was almost shaking. My heart was pounding, and I was experiencing a form of anxiety as I watched the island disappear over the horizon and again when we approached the docks on the mainland.

Soon we were on the highway and headed for the Ohio Turnpike where I faced a culture shock that changed me forever. The first day alone I saw a train, busses, traffic lights, and a freeway! For hours we traveled at speeds of 70 MPH, fences were a blur and telephone poles went by like a picket fence. I spent so much time looking out the window that they nicknamed me Dog – because to them I looked like a dog that rides in a car with his head out the window. That became my nickname until I went to Ann Arbor a few years later – it then became "Deputy Dog" from the popular cartoon of the day.

Woodstock was about 450 miles from the island. Soon after passing through a city called Bethel N.Y., and just before Woodstock, we came upon a farm. Though we were 2 days early there were already hundreds of cars. It wasn't hard to figure out that there was going to be more people than they had estimated. By the second day New York freeways were closed, and there were an estimated 450,000 people there.

As we entered the fenced area and gave up our tickets the first thing I saw was these towers of erected scaffold that were full of speakers. I had never seen speakers that big, nor did I have any idea that there could even be that many of them. I heard a variety of announcements blaring from the P.A.'s. There was so much to take in and I was completely overwhelmed. One member of our group – Timmy – had some blotter acid that looked like a postcard and was called "4-Way." You just tore off a perforated square or two and ate it. In the midst of all this I was now hallucinating, and the colors, the trails, and the sounds became beyond surrealistic. I met this girl named Debbie. She was 17, about 5'5" tall and about 105 lbs. She had long dark brown hair that extended far below her waist and she was more than blessed with shape and curves, even beyond the centerfolds of the day. She was more experienced than I at many things. She told Pete and Kate that she would keep an eye on me after they explained who I was and where I had been all my life. Debbie and I spent the whole time together during the festival as I was so high on acid, mescaline, mushrooms, etc. that I swear I could hear the wax melting in my ears.

There was this huge stage and I remember looking up to see performers like Grace Slick and The Jefferson Airplane, Country Joe McDonald and The Fish, Janis Joplin and scores of other musicians. But the best was watching the sun come up on the horizon of the second day to the sound of Jimi Hendrix playing his version of The Star Spangled Banner. To this day this is one of my most significant memories as it

15

actually coincided with the loss of my virginity to Debbie. It was two weeks before my 19th birthday and even though much of my Woodstock adventure is foggy, some memories are complete in detail, color and taste! While I may have a vague memory of the severe rainstorm I will never forget the helicopters bringing in food and portable toilets!

Robert G. Schmidt – Post-Woodstock

The last day of the concert they announced that because of all the drugs at the festival it would be unwise to leave the place with them. It is hard to describe the last day there. Pounds of marijuana were put on smoldering piles of charcoal. People were consuming all the rest of the peyote, mushrooms, acid, MDA and whatever else was there. And then, it was over. A half a million American youths had gathered together for peace, love, and music, protesting the war in Vietnam and there was not a single act of violence. The federal government was shocked in a way that would affect the assembly of masses of the people from that day on. Little did we know that the tragedy at Kent State was just over the horizon. That the "powers that be" would try to prevent these huge gatherings of people unless they were in complete control, and that the execution of civilians was a way of enforcing their control, using a propaganda machine to justify their actions.

Many people hitchhiked to the festival, and so the day that we all left there were all kinds of arrangements made to accommodate people getting home. As it turned out I was going to drive Grady's 63 Chevy convertible back with 9 people in it. Grady was a friend of Pete's, and was going to ride back in the truck with this girl he met who was looking for a ride back to Ann Arbor. We filled the trunk with our gear and put the top down. 3 in the front seat, 3 in the back seat, and 3 riding up where the top folded down.

The traffic was stop and go at a snails pace, but by the time we got north to the Ohio-Pennsylvania turnpike things were moving at a reasonable rate. Halfway through Pennsylvania it became dark, and around 10pm I was pulled over by Pennsylvania State Troopers.

The trooper came up to the driver's door and asked for my license. I obliged and he then noticed I was wearing kaleidoscope sunglasses. I was still up on LSD, and when he looked through them he asked how I could possibly see. I told him that it was not a problem, but without them I wasn't sure how many troopers were with him. He totally lost his composure and proceeded to give me a field sobriety test - which of course I passed. I wasn't drunk. He then returned the glasses to me, I put them on and he asked me how many fingers he had up. I said three, which was correct. He just shook his head and mumbled something under his breath. Then, he informed me that I was pulled over because my headlights were painted blue. He asked where we were coming from and we told him "Woodstock." As it turned out we were just one of many cars coming from that "damn hippie festival" with blue headlights. He told us to scrape the paint off and then we could go. There we were, 9 acid tripping hippies trying to scrape blue paint off of 4 headlights with quarters. That was more than one pressed shirt, Smoky the Bear hat, one way sunglasses wearing Pennsylvania Trooper could handle and he took off. The rest of the trip back to the island was uneventful compared to that.

The fact that is most significant here is that I left the island completely knowledgeable of my whereabouts and surroundings as a mariner of the Great Lakes. I then entered into the world, at its pace with all of its sights, sounds and smells. In just a few days I acquired a new base of knowledge, survived it and returned home safely with a new mindset and consciousness of the true world that exists outside of our comfortable parameters. Yes I survived it, but I would never be the same again. The horizon looked different now with each sunset, and the island seemed incredibly small.

1970 Bowling Green & Kent State

After Woodstock came Labor Day Weekend. It was always an eventful weekend because I celebrated my birthday (Aug 31), Labor Day, and the last major tourist weekend closing the season. There was only one more weekend to celebrate before winter, and that would not be until we harvested the grapes and had the annual wine festival. It was a different more select crowd compared to the Labor Day crowd. Soon the island would be a ghost town. You could hear the wind blow. Autumn would turn the trees awesome colors of red, orange and yellow. The leaves were windswept and the lake would become restless.

My family, and especially I, were on stand-by for the Coast Guard - most of the navigation aids would be removed rather than lose them to the ice. Should a late season boater or yachtsman run into trouble we were the closest response team and safe haven. We would keep at least one boat on 24 hr. stand-by until the lake froze completely.

When Lake Erie turned solid the winds of the northeast would scream across her like a hawk with sub-zero temperatures that would tear at your lungs like needles with each breath. Sailboats were traded for iceboats, and our economy was now dependent on the ice fishing business. I worked as a guide taking care of a dozen or more fishing shanties, which were small cabins, built of wood and canvas for ice fishermen. They had a small coal stove and a large hole in the floor to fish through the ice.

I rented an apartment over the general store, and during the winter when I was not working I would play my drums with my headphones hooked up to my stereo. I only had a few albums, The Stones, The Doors, Jefferson Airplane, Velvet Underground, Steppenwolf, Bob Dylan and of course my favorite – Iron Butterfly's "Inagaddadavida." I played that 17 minute drum solo over and over and over again until my fingers would blister and bleed. By the end of the winter I could mouth every note or play the whole solo perfectly with two sticks on anything. It was permanently etched in my mind as it is still today.

A few people I had met during the Woodstock trip came and visited me for a week at a time. I told them, "To appreciate the island you need to visit during the winter when there are no tourists." I introduced them to skating long distances, sail-skating with a hand held sail, ice boating and most of all – the skill required to drive across Lake Erie in a car without getting wet. This is the skill that my great uncles used to become financially independent during Prohibition by running Canadian whiskey into the U.S.

In the evenings we would sit around the fire and they would talk about A2. That is what they called Ann Arbor, Michigan. They were enrolled at the university there, and I learned of social changes and movements that were rooting there. Cultural change was in the air, we now had the 18-year-old vote, and politics were being reformed by the massiveness of a co-operative youth vote. We quickly realized that despite our racial, musical or social backgrounds and differences, we all had a common denominator, which was that we all despised the current system of things, and we held the keys to make that change in our hands. We would organize, we would speak out, we would be counted as voters and make the change. After all it was our generation that was doing the killing and dying in Vietnam. We paid the price in our own blood, and that was soon to be the case in May at Kent State University in Ohio.

In the meantime independent thinking, collective organizing and brotherhood were the norm for the day. It was a time of thinking outside the box, questioning authority, and listening to our conscience telling us it was wrong to kill. In spite of religious leaders promoting the war, we knew that God hated the shedding of innocent blood, the destruction of what He created. So we followed our hearts and fell away from formalized religion that had sold us for a few pieces of silver. We separated from religious doctrine based on "Do as we say, not as we do," "silent, unquestioning obedience," "be seen, not heard." We pursued new paths to find a change in what we knew was wrong. We hungered for knowledge based on accurate truths. The future would be ours – that is if we did not get killed in the process.

Then in May that is exactly what happened. We were all at Bowling Green University for a week of peaceful war protest. It was great, we all marched, carried signs and were joined by many students from the schools. Afterwards we got in our vehicles, and some boarded buses, and we drove to Kent State. The rally was already underway, and we were so excited that with the addition of our group there would be hundreds of us. As we entered the parking lots at the north end of the campus we met other students from Ohio State of Columbus and we assembled together. Then it happened. We heard the sound of gunshots, and then an eerie silence for a moment, and then there was a burst of pandemonium. Four students had been shot dead and others were wounded. The news said we ran away. The truth is we did run, but not away. We ran to the scene and the National Guard figured out quickly that they did not have enough bullets to kill all of us. They ran away. They claimed that students threw rocks at them. It was a grassy campus, there were not any rocks anywhere to be found. As the National Guardsmen ran for their lives, riots broke out, and we were throwing bottles and bricks and anything we could find, pry, or pick up at them. Finally the dean of the university calmed us with common sense as we were destroying our own halls of education. To this day I hold within an anger that has never subsided. I only keep it concealed, and under control. At times it does surface, and it cripples my creativity and my compassionate nature.

The summer of 1970 became a time of healing inspired by Crosby, Stills, Nash and Young's recording of *Ohio: "Tin Soldiers and Nixon's coming, we're finally on our own. This summer I heard the drumming, four dead in Ohio."* That was too close to home and that Fall I left the island. I had lived in paradise, but there was a greater need in the real world, and I wanted to be a soldier in the "guitar army." My motto became: "It is better to burn out than to fade away."

As September rolled around I packed a couple of bags into my 1962 Austin Healy Sprite and headed to the mainland. I would stay with friends in Toledo until I got my sense of direction. I knew not where I was going in life, but in blind faith I knew that unless I took those steps down the path, how else would I find where it would lead to? Rather than procrastinate over the variables, I took the steps.

A2

When I got to Toledo, Ohio I stayed at Jeff Bykowski's place. It was like a commune, and there was a rock & roll jam session every night, as most of these new friends were musicians. I got a hold of Pete & Kate and would occasionally go to their place. I was dating a girl named Cindy then. Cindy was a longtime friend of Kate's. They had gone to high school together.

Around Thanksgiving I was hanging out in Ann Arbor Michigan at the university. College students nicknamed the town, "A2," or "The Square," as in A square, or A to the second power. On State Street there were many head shops and I would do leatherwork and sell my finished pieces there. I made a top hat just like the one the Mad Hatter wore in "Alice in Wonderland." Mine was made out of alligator skin and it soon became my trademark. It was very useful for hiding our stash in at events we attended.

The "Mad Hatter"

When there were open-air concerts on the diag (campus center) I would do security. The nickname Deputy Dog really stuck.

Security was not what it is today. My job was to spot undercover narcotics agents and then single them out to the reporter for the campus newspaper, the Ann Arbor Sun. They would take pictures of the "narcs," then publish complete histories of them, their arrest records and home addresses in the next issue of the newspaper. That way people would know to be wary of them, and they would become useless. Understand that in Michigan at that time John Sinclair got 10 years for 2 joints. That is where the term "ten for two" came from in the guitar army.

Cannabis Cowboy

I started spending so much time in A2 that I moved to a place just outside of Manchester. There was an old farm on Highway 50, and it put me between the Irish Hills and The Square. I had long since up-graded my old Austin Healy Sprite for a Porsche. It was better suited for "running" the old farm roads. Cindy and I had parted ways and I had a new girlfriend named Eileen. She was much younger than I, but was very advanced for her age. At 5'4" and around 100 lbs. and long blond hair she was quite a handful. Full of a spirit for adventure and a more than desirable body, she had the abilities to get whatever she set her mind to. She really loved our smuggling business, and wanted to become an airplane pilot. We had a couple of Doberman Pinschers named Affy & Gypsy. The dogs were the equivalent of our children, and they served their purpose at the farm providing company and protection.

As Congress had lowered the voting age from 21 to 18 years of age, we (the students) formed a political party and successfully elected a few students to the City Council. Then one night, when a few council members were out sick, we voted in a new marijuana law. Marijuana possession would be only a $5 fine – a ticket you could pay by mail. Any amount of pot inside the city limits was only a $5 fine. Things were changing quickly now, and A2 became a distribution point for weed in the Tri-State area.

It was like Prohibition and bootlegging all over again. It didn't take much to out-run a Dodge Diplomat driven by the Michigan State police, and all of our vehicles were equipped with a new electronic device called a radar detector. Soon there were Porches, Ferraris, Maseratis and Jaguars everywhere. New four wheel drive pickup trucks with camper shells were the tool for bulk loads. You could carry about a hundred pounds in a sports car, but if you needed to transport more you could get up to 3,500 pounds in a 4 x 4 with a camper. We still had long hair, we still wore blue jeans but everyone was wearing turquoise, silver, gold chains and Rolexes. The day of the poor hippie was gone. Ann Arbor looked like a page out of the Fury Freak Brothers comic book, crossed with Robert Mitchum's "Tobacco Road" movie. Everybody looked like Freewheelin Franklin or Fat Freddie. Soon, though, this was about to change. We were drawing way too much attention on a national level.

At my farm just outside of Saline, Michigan there was a huge tin barn. It was all open inside with huge doors - much like a warehouse. The building was big enough to drive an 18-wheel tractor-trailer rig in, and still had room for 20 pickup trucks. This was perfect for unloading a large truck of marijuana, and re-distributing it to smaller vehicles. We worked three days a month at this, and the rest of the time we grew sunflowers on the property for the seeds. This provided a financial income for the farm and a visible cover for our enterprise.

The winter months were spent flying hovercrafts for Skim Air Corporation out of Perrysburg, Ohio. My close friend Don Thomas (D.T.) and I took this job to fly demonstrations for the company, and to test fly prototypes for the sole purpose of being able to fly across Lake Erie into Canada when the lake was frozen. On ice, a hovercraft could cruise in excess of 100 MPH and travel over ice that was only 1/4 inch thick without breaking it or leaving a trail. You had to be a little nutty to operate a vehicle that could take you into terrain that you could not walk or swim back from. If we broke down – we were stuck – that is why we flew in pairs. These hovercrafts would provide a path to our hash connection across the lake that was outside the box, so to speak. As part of our job with Skim Air we also had to take trips flying all over the United States from Florida to Norfolk, Virginia, flying demonstrations to secure funding for the company, so that they could continue research and development. That included demos for the military. We had security clearances to naval bases, and learned a lot about military surveillance and security, but most of all - protocol. This would be an invaluable asset later on in my life.

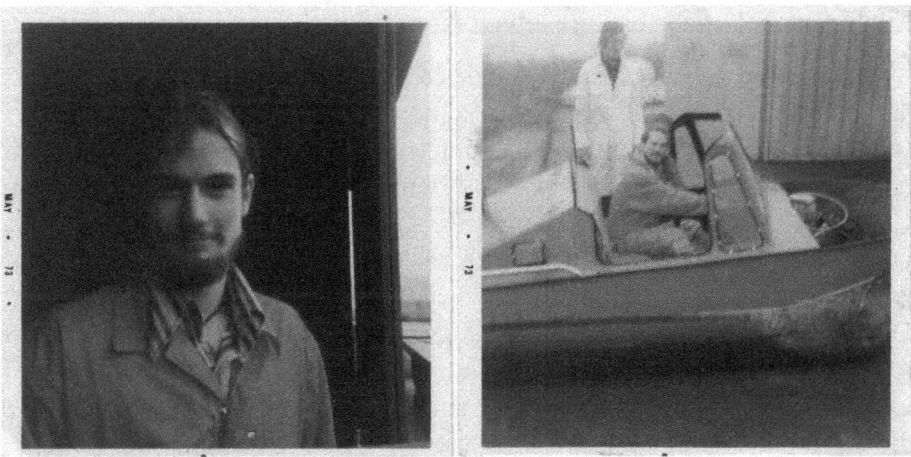

Robert and D.T. preflight a hovercraft

Cannabis Cowboy

While at the University of Michigan I was able to use the chemistry department to make honey oil. This was a product that I made that provided the maximum concentration of THC with each inhale possible. I used an extraction process on a pound of Afghanistan primo hashish and isolated the THC molecule, which could then be smoked with indirect heat in a glass pipe. It allowed the consumer to intake doses of THC that were at a minimal 10 times the intake of conventional joint smoking. It was a clear, odorless, slightly amber product with the consistency of maple syrup. Even drug sniffing dogs cannot detect it, if it is the real McCoy. No one knew what it was, and I was able to sell it over the counter in headshops with the glass pipe and instructions from the "Psychedelic Ranger." Life was good, but that was soon to come to an end.

On May 9th, 1975, the Friday before Mother's Day, in Holland, Ohio, the feds raided D.T.'s place - seizing a pound of Thai sticks and 20,000 hits of LSD. I had met D.T. through Cindy and we became good friends, and still are to this day. He and I flew the hovercrafts together and shared interests in cars along with Thai sticks and honey oil. My ex-girlfriend, Cindy, her sister, D.T. and Chris, his wife, plus many more were taken into custody. I was in shock, how could this have happened?

As it turned out, Don was (unknowingly) dealing with an undercover federal agent named John Graetz. This had been going on for quite a while and they had a good case against him. They were also looking for me, but they didn't know where to look. Don's driving skills on Michigan back roads had prevented them from tailing him to my farm.

I consulted friends that were not caught up in this mess, and it was agreed that we needed to generate some serious cash - and really fast. I was still at large and could maneuver, so we formed a group to make it happen. The team consisted of: Victor, an exchange student from Colombia, South America, Danny, the nephew of a powerful Teamsters Union official who could help with trucking, Ray, an economics major who kept us organized, Pete who had some money to use for a boat, David, who was into electronics, and myself, an excellent mariner that would be the Captain of the boat. Our plan was to run a load of Colombian marijuana from South America, and that is exactly what we did.

My skills as a captain were limited to navigating Lake Erie. Now I was about to travel across the Gulf of Mexico into the Caribbean, and to a country that I had never been to before. Then I would pick up a load of marijuana, and return it to trucks that would be waiting to get loaded to transport it back to Michigan. It all sounded simple enough. Yeah right! The chances of professionals accomplishing this under a legal endeavor were not likely to be successful. But we had one advantage: we were naive and full of optimism - and there was no one to say it couldn't be done.

June, 1975 – RED CLOUD

We took off for Florida, and I bought an old Desco shrimp boat for $55k cash from some Cubans. It was around the 1st of June, and it was hot and muggy in Miami. The name of the boat was Red Cloud, after the great American Indian chief. She was an old Desco fishing boat that had not changed in design for the last 30 years. It was a proven design that had successfully taken fishermen to remote areas of the Caribbean for many years, in any weather, and brought them and their catch back to port safely.

Accommodations were spartan, but the boat had the basic requirements for our purpose: a cargo hold, huge fuel tanks, bunks, refrigeration and a stove. No toilet, no shower. The only thing that remotely resembled a shower was a salty waterfall that could be jury rigged from a pump and a 2-inch hose. The toilet was hanging your ass over the rail and holding on. In fact, in heavy weather you didn't have to wipe – the ocean swells did that for you when the boat would bury itself in the trough - you needed both hands anyway just to keep from falling overboard.

We loaded up with about 10 shopping carts full of groceries and 20-5 gallon water cooler bottles, 15,000 gallons of diesel fuel, charts, cigarettes, rolling papers and yes, a few firearms. We headed out of the harbor in Miami, and then changed our course to the south - and began an incredible journey that would change the course of all our lives forever.

This was an intense amount of responsibility for me as I was now in the big leagues. I was more than confident of handling Lake Erie, but now I had to master the open oceans. I was still hooking up radios and setting up my navigation station while we were already underway. I did not sleep for the first couple of days until I was past Key West, Florida, where we changed our course to the west. This would be my last radar plot of America for a while. We were *en route* to the Yucatan Straits, a southern passage between Yucatan and Colombia that would head us south to Colombia. This would be the longest time I ever ran a boat without seeing land. There were thoughts going through my mind and most of them started with, "What if..." I had no way of being prepared in the event of disaster, as I had no idea of what could be possible. Luckily by the third day I burned out and got some much needed sleep. When I awoke I was watching a beautiful sunset, and remembered that I was free, and some of my close friends were in jail. I had to pull it together, and set about to do just that. I divided the time into four six-hour watches so that two men would be on watch at a time. One at the wheel in the pilothouse, and one for the deck who would be a lookout and make occasional inspections to the engine room and the cargo hold. I would take the midnight to 6am watch, as that would be the most vulnerable time for a collision at sea - and we were in the shipping lanes that were full of gigantic container ships and tankers. They could run us down and they wouldn't even know it.

On the fifth day, right after the evening meal, I was smoking a joint, looking out the galley door and admiring the red sunset. We were surging peacefully through swells, and I was thinking of how the Red Cloud was settling into the trip and not rolling so much. It was an improvement over her usual roly-poly ride, when I felt that the sea seemed to be higher to us.

I looked over the side and sure enough, I could not see her water line. It was under water. I ran to the engine room and it was full of water. We were sinking, and this all happened in less than an hour! We were taking on some serious water, and I had to find the leak quick. The water level in the engine room was just inches short of the air intake of the Caterpillar main engine. If the main engine sucked in water it would bend the rods from hydro locking the cylinders. Then it would be a one-way trip to Davy Jones' Locker.

I alerted the crew, and proceeded to jump into the water in the engine room to find the leak. I was sure that if water was coming in that quick I would be able to feel it. The rest of the crew wanted to abandon ship. I wasn't going to get into a rubber boat in the middle of the ocean while this boat hadn't sunk yet. As I was swimming around under the surface of the water I could feel cold water coming from where the propeller shaft entered the stuffing box. The Red Cloud had spit out her shaft packing, and the rotation of the shaft was acting like a pump - filling the boat full of water. I surfaced, and crawled up on deck to explain the situation to the rest of the crew. I ran to the pilothouse to idle the engine and to put her in neutral, and grabbed a coil of packing. I then ran back to the engine room, slipped a crescent wrench in my belt, bit the coil of packing in my teeth, and jumped back into the water. I swam down behind the main engine and transmission, and felt my way to the stuffing box. I started to undo the bolts on each side of the collar, and to slide the collar back toward the transmission flange. I had to come up for another breath of air and return to the task at hand. The water was coming in with more force now that the collar was out of the way, and I was having trouble pushing the packing in. It took three tries, and I only succeeded by using the collar to hold it as I inched the coil around a little at a time - forcing the packing into the gland. I could only get one bolt on with just a few threads before I ran out of breath. I had to resurface before I could finish the second bolt, and tighten down the gland.

After that I had the boys put the main engine in gear and throttle her up, as I engaged the emergency pump that was operated by the power take-off on the front of the Caterpillar. This was a six-inch line that went from directly into the bilge and through this huge pump and then up to the deck. I was covered with oil, acid, fuel and whatever had been under the main engine all those years, but the good part was that we were no longer sinking. And the bilge was now clean. I took a shower from a two-inch hose of saltwater and Joy dishwashing liquid as the sun disappeared below the horizon, bringing night upon us. If my crew had any doubts about my abilities at the start of this trip, then I can assure you that this was no longer the case. I had not only proven myself to them while enduring an emergency situation by keeping a cool head and initiating a successful plan of action, but I had also belayed any of my own personal doubts and fears.

Thirteen days from our departure in Miami we were off the coast of Colombia and met with Victor. We loaded up 55,000 pounds of Colombian reefer and proceeded to Marathon Key, Florida to unload it. Everything went unbelievably like clockwork. Dan was waiting with two refrigerated tractor-trailer rigs in Marathon, one was a Peterbilt and the other one a Kenworth. As they headed for Detroit, I took the Red Cloud back to Miami and then, as agreed, headed for Ann Arbor. We all met at the Campus Inn a week later.

We now had the capital to start fixing the mess. We had raised over $900,000 after expenses and were able to help some really good people. I enjoyed the smuggling part so much that I initiated a plan to have everyone put the blame on me, so that they would be released from jail or receive a reduction of their sentence. I would lead the feds on a wild goose chase over the next few years. After all, how could they find me if I was out on the ocean? I might as well keep doing what I was doing as I seemed to have a talent for this type of work, and I was a fugitive anyway, right? So I made another run in the Red Cloud immediately, and then sold her for a faster boat, the Joe Louis.

July, 1975 – Crash & Burn

In July things would change. I had just gotten paid from my last trip, and was traveling east on M50 in my Porsche. Herby, Affy (my Doberman) and I were on our way to see Eileen. I met Herby through a friend of D.T. Herby was about 20 years old at that time, with dark long hair and an independent attitude. He worked for me at the farm taking care of the property, helping with shipments and watching the place in my absence. We were high on life and driving in excess of 100 MPH, sliding through the curves, talking about the trip and our new found fortunes.

Then, from the other direction, a full sized Chevy was straddling the double yellow line, and there was not enough shoulder between the road and guardrail. We hit driver's headlight for driver's headlight. It was like an explosion as the cars were spun into circular orbits. The three of us were shot out of the car. Herby slid under a guardrail, crossed the creek and landed in a freshly plowed cornfield next to Affy. He had a cut over his eye and serious road rash. Affy had a broken leg. I slid for a long way, and then started somersaults eventually coming to a stop. In a state of shock I got up and started back to the car, which was on fire. It was like something out of the Twilight Zone with my ears ringing, the wind blowing and my empty burning car - that smelled of the 16 pounds of Thai sticks that were incinerating in the trunk. I was bewildered. Where was Herby? Where was Affy? Where was the car I hit? Here I am in the middle of nowhere with a burning car, the smell of marijuana and in a strange condition of surrealism. Was I dead? Had I entered another dimension? I called out to Herby and soon he came crawling up over the creek bank. He acknowledged his presence and I told him that he should sit down, that he was in bad shape. He informed me that maybe I should look in the mirror!

The car we hit was in a cornfield on the other side of the road. The driver was in a state of shock with a broken arm. The impact was so severe that three of her car's wheels were missing. The driver's side front wheel and suspension were completely gone. The engine was shoved back and under where the transmission should be. The driveshaft was shoved back through the differential, and stuck out of the back of it like a straw in a tree after a hurricane. The force from that ejected both rear axles complete with wheels and backing plates. When they set the car on the ground at the wrecking yard, Herby had his picture taken with a yardstick to show that both bumpers were on the ground, and the doorpost in the center was raised up 18 inches. That Chevy was almost folded like a pocketknife. My car was crushed to the front wheels, and the front axle was pushed back about 4 inches. The pedals inside the car were pushed back around 2 inches. Velocity over-ruled mass in this case.

We were taken to Tecumseh Michigan County Hospital. When we arrived, the doctor took one look at me, and told me there was nothing he could do for me. Then they went to talk to Herby. I was freaking out. Here I am about to die, no priest, no friends, and they just walked away from me.

After a while Herby came in to see me, and he told me they were going to transport me to St. Joseph's Hospital in Ann Arbor where there was an intensive care trauma unit. But first they had to stabilize me, so I was given an injection of Demerol.

During all this excitement there was some confusion about the dosage of Demerol I was to be given. The nurse questioned the dosage, but was reassured by the doctor to follow the order. They gave me 500mg of Demerol, and she put a piece of tape on me stating, "500mg Demerol," as she was still concerned about dosage.

I was in the ambulance and they started losing me. The paramedics saw the tape and panicked, because they were about to lose me to a drug overdose. They got on the radio to St. Josephs and the hospital was instructing them how to keep me alive. I was vomiting, and they had to vacuum my airways to prevent suffocation (like Jimi Hendrix). The vacuum pump worked off of the engine in the ambulance, and that required that they drive fast, and then coast to create a high amount of vacuum. I owe Herby my life because he was sitting in the front seat of the ambulance throwing $100 bills at the driver to keep going and not lose me. My heartbeat stopped just as we entered the city limits, but Herby kept throwing money at them and would not allow them to quit. They were taking short cuts through parking lots and through a picnic area.

July, 1975 – Crash & Burn

I had been a flat line for over 4 minutes when we arrived at the hospital. I was revived, and woke up in a hospital completely disoriented. Herby was there, Eileen was there, the paramedics were there and I was told the amazing story of what all had happened after I lost consciousness.

After a week in the hospital, and seeing specialist after specialist, I was getting cabin fever. But, most of all, I was afraid the feds would find me there, as I was in no condition to run. I was about to get released - I just didn't know it yet.

Eileen came in one afternoon while I was sleeping and proceeded to crawl in bed with me. She was in the middle of horizontal oral groin massage therapy when a Catholic nun came in to give me my medication. She flipped out and ran down the hall screaming. Next, a Catholic priest came in with my doctors and asked what was going on? I replied that they had brought in a specialist for my back, eyes, internal organs, etc. so I was also checking with a specialist to insure that everything was working properly.

It was determined, in not so many colorful words, that I was well enough to leave for home. I was in need of constant care, and Eileen nursed me back to health. I was in a back brace, my vision was blurry, I had migraine headaches, my left foot was a mess, but I was alive – I was free. I had lost over $80k in cash that burned up in the car. The heat was so intense that it melted my silver and gold jewelry in the glove box into a pool on the floor of the car. The turquoise stones had turned white from the heat, and Affy had a rod in his leg. Boy were we a pair.

The boys had taken up a collection for me, bought me a new Porsche, and there was a half pound of Thai sticks in the back seat. All I needed now was to kick back for some rest & relaxation. Eileen drove me to a rented house in Florida to recuperate, while she went to flying school at Embry Riddle School of Aeronautics in Daytona Beach, Fla. We stayed there until Labor Day weekend, and then we returned to the farm in Michigan.

September, 1975 – Cartagena

It was the start of Indian summer, and Ray came by to drop off the balance of my money from the last trip. He asked if I was well enough to go with him to Texas, and then on to Colombia. Victor and his family down there were having a party and we were all invited. I accepted the invitation, but I informed Ray that I did not have a passport. I also reminded him that I was a fugitive. He reassured me not to worry, and to give him my vital statistics so as to acquire a passport for me under an assumed name. I already had a list of names of relatives from my home town at Put-in-Bay, who had died before they were old enough to start school. I had already acquired their birth certificates. Within a week Ray returned to pick me up to go to the airport and to fly to Texas. He handed me a Diplomatic Passport that had been issued out of Bogotá, Columbia. Ray told me that these passports would allow us to pass right through any customs check-point without being searched. On this trip that would not be necessary, as we would be traveling on a private chartered plane with the rest of the boys from Detroit.

When we landed in Cartagena we were greeted by Victor's younger brother Jaime. He had arranged transportation for all of us to a villa up in the hills overlooking the coast. As we arrived at this place I could not help but notice that the courtyard was filled with exotic European classic cars - from Ferraris, to Porsches and Maseratis to Bentleys. There were some rare American muscle cars such as Cobras and Corvettes. This made quite an impression on me. We got out of the Suburbans, and started walking towards a long winding stone staircase that led up to this incredible mansion. I could hear Victor's arrogant voice greeting us from a balcony above. He had a glass of champagne in one hand and a beautiful blonde on his right arm. It turns out that she was some famous model from Europe. We finally reached him and he introduced us to his parents and his cousins who seemed quite eager to meet us. We were Victor's American friends whose entrepreneurial endeavors were providing a new source of revenue to their already successful enterprises. We were being treated like emissaries of an American corporation. I have to admit that it felt pretty good, as we were accustomed to being discriminated against as hippies in the United States, much like second class citizens. Most of the time I was paranoid of being discovered or questioned about who I was, or what I did for a living. Here it didn't matter.

There was only one real problem here that set us aside from the rest. We were guests in a foreign country who did not speak the language. We had different customs, and we were even accustomed to a different variety of food. It didn't take me too long to get bored, and so I exercised my status as an honored guest to explore this outrageous place. It seems that there were parties or groups of people in every chamber of this villa. I was on the second floor of the atrium when I ran into Jamie. He asked if I was enjoying myself, and also asked why I was up there. So I explained that I was on an adventure exploring the place, and he warned me not to go into the room at the end of the hall as they were some very powerful people that headed up the governing body of families in this part of Columbia. At that he turned and headed off into the direction of some very beautiful women. Well, now I was curious. I could not resist walking past the doorway and at least looking in, and that is exactly what I did. As I was peering in I could hear that they were speaking German, so I asked in my worst German, *"Sprechen zei Duetsche"?*

That was immediately followed by, *"Kommen here!"* I entered. You could here a pin drop. In less than a second German phrases and demands were flying at me, and I was overwhelmed as I only knew a few German phrases at best. It was at this time a man my age with long hair came forward and introduced himself as Alberto Weber in English. I told him that I was Robert Schmidt, a friend of Victor's from America. Alberto translated this to the others, and I was introduced to his father and his uncles, and given a Cuban cigar. Alberto asked what I did with the group of Americans, and I explained that I was a boat captain. It was not long before I heard them saying *"Kapitan un der boot,"* and saw discussions among them while they pointed their fingers in reference to me. Alberto had explained that I was the captain that was successfully completing the recent shipments of theirs. This gave me celebrity status immediately, and with my German name and background I was now at the top of the food chain. Through Alberto we talked for hours about my family and my background - only to discover that these people were the real power brokers. They advised me that I should be very cautious of the Columbians and not to trust them. *Ever.*

September, 1975 – Cartagena

Alberto and I started to become really good friends, but Jaime and Victor were not happy about this. Ray pulled me off to the side to bring this to my attention. It was at this time that Ray and I compared notes, and I introduced him to Alberto. Alberto suggested that we take a ride in the Mercedes 6.3 that he had just had received from Germany. On the way into town Alberto explained that the Colombians that we knew were actually descendants of the Spanish Conquistadors that had invaded and pillaged this country centuries before. They made the indigenous tribes slaves. This put a whole new perspective on the situation. It was at this time that I decided to befriend the Indians of the jungle and the coastal areas where I was working.

We arrived at this sleazy cantina that Alberto frequented on a regular basis. He was well known and liked there, so we felt quite comfortable with the bar maids and the local clientele. We continued our conversation, and soon learned that Alberto's family would rather do business directly with us. With Victor's people there was always a problem with the shipments, or the money. Alberto came right out and called Victor an idiot, and Jamie a weasel. He was surprised that we even got paid, but I attributed that fact to Ray handling all of the money. Victor was just the hook-up. Alberto warned us that Jamie, on the other hand, was crafty, and not to be trusted - in no uncertain terms.

At this time a large Colombian maniac burst into the bar with a sawn-off shot gun screaming ".....PUTA something..." Alberto yelled to get down while grabbing me by my right arm and dragging me off my chair. As I was flipping over to the right I heard the sound of both barrels blasting away - leaving my ears ringing. The couple who was sitting at the table behind us were both on the floor oozing blood. Alberto grabbed Ray and me, and shoved us toward the side entrance, and out into the street. We ran for the car, got in and sped off. Ray and I were in shock, but Alberto was laughing, mumbling in between breathes about adultery being a heavy price if you get caught, and that guy would probably only get a ticket for discharging a fire-arm in a public place.

Speeding through these winding back streets Alberto looked much like an American moonshiner of the forties - shifting, braking, and throwing the wheel from one direction to the other. The big sedan was drifting around corners, pitching from one side of the street to the other, while an occasional chicken slammed into the windshield in a burst of feathers. As I was shouting to Ray, who was in the back seat, Alberto asked if I had been hit as I was incessantly scratching my left knee. I answered no. He then asked why my fingers were red. I looked at them and sure enough he was right. So I rolled up my left pant leg and sure enough blood was trickling down from just below my kneecap. I guess that when Alberto flipped me over, my left leg swung up high enough to catch one pellet from the shotgun blast. I never did get that pellet out and to this very day you can see where it entered by the grey-green dot on my left knee. It would be a souvenir that constantly reminded me that I needed to be aware of my surroundings at all times. I often joked about Alberto being such an asset for us, and how fortunate we were to have met him. After all, the day I met him was also the day I got shot!

From that day on, Ray and I knew that we now had a good contact, and even more - an ally that we could trust. As time went on Alberto would prove to be a valuable member of our operation, who not only had skills and a mutual interest for our success, but also unquestionable integrity. He would be more than just a liaison between his family and us. His credibility would open the path for me to establish a network of indigenous tribes that would benefit from our mutual endeavors, by serving as a chain of out-posts that ran from Medellín to Riohacha. A blueprint model of the Knights Templar, during the Crusades of the 12th century, that extended from Europe to the Middle East. This system would provide us with provisions, security, and intelligence over the next couple of years. It would create a communal bond between us and the indigenous residents based on a foundation of empathy, respect, and necessity.

October, 1975: The JOE LOUIS

It was a hot Michigan morning and I was dreading another uncomfortable day in the heat. I was wearing this "turtle" -- a sophisticated, immobilizing back-brace -- due to the serious car accident I had in July. The silence of the farm was disturbed by the sound of a Triumph GT6 coming up the gravel driveway. It was Herby. As he got out of the car, I greeted him with a monster joint soaked in honey oil. As he took a hit, he handed me "the envelope." Inside was the usual: a plane ticket, hotel reservation, and $5,000. Someone had arranged a meeting.

I realized immediately that something had gone wrong. I was supposed to have six months to recuperate from the accident, as I could hardly get around with four fused vertebrae, a dislocated neck and a shattered left foot. I couldn't even see straight from the trauma of the impact. My last visit to Colombia I got shot.

In spite of my physical condition, I had Herby take me to the airport, and I headed for New Orleans to find out what was going on. At a minimum, I could provide some advice. After all, my crew was off doing who knows what, and we wouldn't contact each other until after the Christmas holidays.

When I arrived at "LE'BOOZE" bar on Bourbon Street in the French Quarter, I was greeted by Ray and Dan. It was like a family reunion. The joy of the moment soon subsided and the atmosphere became very somber. They informed me that the last load did not "hook up," Chris was missing and another load was ready. We were "backed up."

They asked me if I was well enough to run down to "Del Diablo" near Riohacha with another boat and pick up both loads. I asked them where would I find my crew on such short notice? They didn't even know their whereabouts, but said Captain Larry's crew would load both boats, and they would provide me with two deckhands to help me handle my boat. Larry was a longtime fisherman out of Marathon Key, Florida. He had been a shrimper all of his life. His boat was a family business, and he was well known in the small community as a generous and kind individual.

I chartered a twin-engine Cessna to fly me to Marathon, where I kept the Joe Louis stashed at Pinnella Sea Foods not far from Larry's boat. This was the perfect place to hide a 65' Desco lobster boat - like the one on the front cover of the famous Jimmy Buffet album. She had a V-1710 Cummins diesel, and was built for speed and endurance. I could carry enough fuel to cruise 6,000 miles at 275 miles a day in any weather conditions.

Two days later I met Hal and Mark, who were sent down by Ray and Dan to help me run my boat by taking wheel watches when I slept. It all sounded like it could work, so I agreed to lead the trip. We fueled and provisioned the Joe Louis, and Larry's boat and got ready to set out. Larry would leave at dawn, and I would leave in the evening so as not to arouse any suspicions. Most fishermen are protective of the whereabouts of their fishing grounds.

Capt. Larry's boat, the Dudley, was a Carolina boat about 95' in length. They are huge and built for the seas of Cape Hatteras, the "graveyard of the Atlantic." He had a crew of 7 men and could distance about the same as my boat. We agreed to meet at Latitude 25 degrees and Longitude 80 degrees, which put us due east of Marathon, Florida - about 70 miles offshore. It was a tricky feat of navigation, but a common practice of smugglers to ensure a covert rendezvous.

We then headed southwest for the Yucatan Channel, and after two days we headed southeast towards the Rosalind Banks and onward to Colombia. During this time, to my dismay, I learned that the sea-faring skills of Mark and Hal only amounted to some ski-boats on Lake Michigan! Nevertheless, they were learning quite quickly and knew the basics of boating, and not to fall overboard. They had enough skills to take a wheel watch, and enough common sense to wake me if there was a problem.

Two days after we changed course in the Yucatan Straits, the barometer began to fall like a Japanese Zero during the Marianas Turkey Shoot. In all my years at sea, I have never seen mercury drop that fast without breaking glass. Hurricane Clara was in full swing near the Windward Passage, and we were being whipped by her spin-off.

The waves were around 40 feet tall, from the bottom of the trough to the crest. I loved this kind of weather, because the least of our worries was the Coast Guard. Hurricanes were an excellent way for smugglers to use cover if they were equipped and experienced enough to dance with them. One does not "drive" through these conditions, but rather finesses one's boat in a way to work with Mother Nature. Waves hit at about 7 pounds per gallon of water, and an average wave consists of tens of thousands of gallons. A boat could be crushed under these conditions, should there be a lapse in judgment or reflex.

My boat, a Desco, has round bilges, and she likes to roll around in the seas like a duck in the water. Waves would crash over her, roll her on her sides, and we would pop up shedding water off our back. To some it is like a rollercoaster ride at an amusement park. To others, it can be a terrifying experience…and this was to be the case with Mark and Hal, as they had never seen a wave over 4 feet before.

Meanwhile, Capt. Larry and the Dudley were running flat and stable, and his crew was experiencing a much more stable ride. Mark and Hal were no use to me, as they had become very sick. They were dehydrated from throwing up, and fatigued from going without sleep. Larry and I agreed to transfer them to his boat for a while. This was a very dangerous maneuver in these conditions. If the boats hit each other during the transfer of crew, we could both sink. I decided we would bring the boats nose-to-nose and let them jump across on the rise of a wave. As Larry headed his boat into the weather, I maneuvered the Joe Louis around to approach with a following sea. The chines of my boat were round, and would give less resistance to the lift of the waves. This would allow me to approach Larry's boat without being pitched into him, which could split our stems - destroying both boats. Larry put his boat in neutral, and I gingerly brought the Joe Louis up to the Dudley. Soon we were close enough that both boats were rising and falling together on the same wave in perfect timing. The boys stepped across with less than a foot of separation. With this done Larry and I threw our boats into reverse to separate them as quickly as possible before a freak wave could slam us together. I prudently do not recommend this type of maneuver to anyone, at any time, under any conditions, but I must admit that it worked out quite well.

Now that we had completed that circus act, I resumed our course to Colombia. Larry stayed about 8 miles behind me, following and tracking me on his radar. We were in communication by radio, as David had modified our VHF's with "split crystals," and only we could hear our conversations. On low range, we were broadcasting on less than one watt, and our transmitting range was only 15 nautical miles.

This all seemed to be working well until nightfall, when Hal and Mark were to come back aboard my boat. There was a full moon, and the waves had increased in height due to the lunar effect. It was not going to be possible to bring the boats together under these conditions. Prudent judgment led Larry and I to agree to abandon the option. We would try again at dawn.

I settled in for a wild ride that night, as the waves had exceeded 40 feet. An occasional rogue wave even went over 65 feet, which was the entire length of the Joe Louis! Around 2300 hours (11pm) I was taking lists and rolls that were exceeding the capabilities of my antique auto-pilot. A couple of times I had to override it, since my boat, during the surf down the wave fronts, was listing over so badly that her rudder was ineffective, and she would try to spin-out. It was like riding a 65 foot surfboard in a tsunami. My heart was pounding from the adrenalin rush while Tchaikovsky's "Nutcracker Suite" blasted out of the stereo speakers in a complete synchronous pattern with the waves and spray. It was outrageous, and it gave my grave situation some surrealistic comic relief.

Then it happened. I was hit by a rogue wave from astern that lifted the Joe Louis almost perpendicular, and we were surfing down a wave at such a steep angle that we were exceeding our hull speed and she was pushing water from the bow like a large moustache. The autopilot jammed, she spun out and buried her starboard rail into the trough, tripping her into a barrel roll. I was pitched out of the captain's chair, flew across the pilothouse and crashed through the wooden door, slamming into her bulwarks on deck and held there by my back brace. That stupid "turtle" saved my life! The next thing I knew, we were upright and cruising along in the trough like nothing was wrong. That was just an illusion from the shock. I freed myself, ran into the pilothouse, disengaged the autopilot and tried to visually assess the damage.

The Joe Louis and I were in serious trouble -- everything was torn loose helter-skelter. Every drawer had flown open, emptying its contents all over. Every cupboard and compartment was emptied out onto the
44

floor. Canned goods, mattresses, ship's stores and all my electronics were in a tangled mess in every direction. I had taken on a lot of water, but the main engine was still humming away like nothing had happened. I was still underway. No radios, no navigation aids, no lights…yet I was still running. I grabbed a chart and started to form a plan. Capt. Larry and I were now separated. I could see him, but I could not call him. I was on my own.

I was about 500 miles from Kingston, Jamaica, so I set a course due east, knowing that I could make repairs there with minimal or no questions asked. Just two and a half more days under these conditions, and then I could get some rest.

Hurricane Clara was winding down now. The sun was out, the winds moderate and the seas were no longer dark monsters -- just large, gradual swells. The Joe Louis had a good feel about her, so I just sat back and ate crackers and drank Kool-Aid for two and a half days, while steering with my feet, listening to some Bob Marley tunes on the remains of the 8 track player. I was in no hurry. The damage was done, and all I had to do was pace myself to Jamaica and think of a good story for the authorities.

After a couple of days, I entered the harbor at Kingston at around 1 am. I proceeded to the Customs dock and maneuvered the Joe Louis up to the wharf. As I was tying her up, truckloads of Jamaican police and military came screeching up and jumped on board with automatic weapons pointing at me. I immediately informed them that they had jumped onto a boat that was actually sinking. When they saw how much water there was in the engine room, they abandoned the boat even faster than they had jumped onto it. Although I was still holding my hands up at gunpoint, I couldn't help laughing out loud. In fact, it broke the tension. When the inspector asked why I was laughing, I explained that I found it ironic that after all I had survived over the last couple of days, I was about to sink at the dock in a safe harbor at gunpoint. The inspector holstered his pistol and said I could put my arms down. He offered me a Dunhill cigarette and asked if I needed a drink. I accepted his offer, and began to explain why and how I was in his harbor.

His officers searched the boat and found nothing illegal, but they were wondering where my crew was - they had found Mark and Hal's passports and belongings in their cabin. I told them about the seas, and putting them on Capt. Larry's boat. It was a little too fantastic to believe, until one of his officers asked us to go down into the engine room. From the oil and grease streaks on the ceiling, it was confirmed that the Joe Louis had, in fact, rolled 360 degrees.

In spite of this, I was under "house arrest." My passport was seized until I could confirm the whereabouts of Mark and Hal, but I was free to roam about the island. I took the Joe Louis across the harbor to Port Royal in Morgan's Harbor, and rented a suite at the Morgan's Harbor Hotel. I called Ray's girlfriend and told her what happened, and then fell asleep on the bed. I was tired and drunk and hurting.

I am not sure how long I was asleep, but it was quite a while. The next thing I knew, someone was trying to wake me up - it was Dan and Ray! They said Larry had contacted them by radio, and had given me up for lost. They were so relieved when Ray's girlfriend had relayed my message to him. Larry and the Dudley were on their way to Port Royal and would be there in a few days. Repairs were already started on the Joe Louis. There was nothing for me to do but burn some Ganja spliffs and drink Jamaican rum...and get some rest.

Soon the Dudley arrived, Mark, Hal, and Captain Larry confirmed my story to the inspector. Ray paid off a few officials to satisfy any inquiries about my boat, me, why and for what. That's the way it was back in the day. For ten thousand dollars here and there, you could buy silence and fix things. A few pounds of money and a handshake were a binding agreement in the Caribbean, and everyone was happy.

Within a fortnight, all the repairs were done and both boats were re - provisioned. We all set sail again for Del Diablo, bound together by a common goal, mutual reward, and a new-found respect for each other, based on endurance under trial.

It was a magnificent red sunset in Morgan's Harbor at Port Royal, Jamaica. With the repairs and refitting of the Joe Louis completed, I set off again on my original trip, accompanied by Capt. Larry on the Dudley. Not wanting to appear suspicious, we agreed to take alternate courses and separate as soon as we cleared the channel entrance buoy.

I headed west with the Joe Louis and Larry took the Dudley south. We would meet again on the high seas just off the Rosalind Banks in about two and a half days.

46

From there, we would tandem down to the "Lion's Paw" to confirm the load was ready and then head east, hugging the coast, to Del Diablo.

The Lion's Paw was a massive plateau made up of five "fingers" of land that jutted out into the ocean, about 50 miles west of Santa Marta. From the ocean, it looked like a lion's paw, and so that's what I called it. No one else would know where, or what, I was talking about unless they were also in the trade. The cliffs were steep and they dropped right into the ocean with no significant beach. They were surrounded by large submerged rocks, and there were no accurate maps of the submerged dangers, other than the charts I had made over the previous years. It was my sanctuary, as even the locals feared the area. It was marked on commercial charts as a place to be avoided by prudent mariners who valued the safety of their vessels and crew. This was a very dangerous place to be in heavy weather, as there was no protection from surge and currents. The fact was simple—if you lost power, your boat would be dragged through the rocks and your crew could only abandon ship to beat the grinding, merciless cliffs.

It was my kind of place. Nobody wanted it, no one would follow you in there, and radio communication was limited by the line of sight. We didn't need to worry about anyone "listening in," especially on the low band at just 1 watt.

Our contact would sit and wait on the ocean face of the cliff and he could look down for miles in either direction to see whether we were there on time. When we hooked up with our contact by radio, we would run 150 miles west to Del Diablo and be greeted by him and scores of cayucas (dug-out canoes). The cayucas had contracts with us to bring the cargo off the beach, so that we could load it in deep water. Being out in the open helped us so that our radar was more effective. It allowed us a better opportunity to escape, should any Venezuelan gunboats try to pin us in to collect a bounty on us. The DEA offered a $10,000 reward to them and, on top of that, they would get to keep our boats. This was a "dead or alive" bounty, which usually emphasized "dead." This eliminated the need for paperwork and political red tape. Remember that nobody knew that we were even in those waters. The thought of spending the rest of our lives in a Colombian prison encouraged us to continue a fight until victory or until they pried our cold, dead fingers off our weapons. We had pledged together to go down with the ship rather than surrender.

As we headed for Del Diablo, we encountered some of my "regulars" fishing offshore, and they hailed us as we were passing. They knew why we were there. We brought them on board and took their cayucas in tow.

We spoke in a unique dialogue made up of Arawak, Caribe Indian, and Pidgin English, which we had invented because they do not and will not communicate in Spanish. Greetings were exchanged, as well as blessings of camaraderie and respect, followed by news of their families (mostly births and deaths) and information about the stability of the political climate. They hated the Spanish Colombians, since they were the indigenous residents who had been conquered and enslaved by the Jesuits and Conquistadores a couple of hundred years before. I didn't trust the Colombians either, so I got along quite well with these fishermen. It made for an interesting co-dependent relationship. They needed things like medical supplies, tools, blankets and generators, which I would bring them in mass quantities.

You see, they had no use for money.

There were very few stores in the area at this time. Barter was the basis of their economy. In return, they provided me with intelligence about DEA activity and the cartel movements, and they were my eyes and ears during critical times when we were loading. It was their turf, after all. They knew every rock, snail and tree branch on a first-name basis. Their survival instincts were acutely honed from centuries of being hunted, enslaved and abused by the Spanish descendants we all called "Colombianos."

They also hated the DEA and the U.S. Block-Ops that were operating in the area even more. These Indians were treated with less respect than animals, and it was not uncommon for women and children to be executed in the effort to extract information from the tribesmen. The fact of the matter is this – the atrocities credited to Pablo Escobar were carried out by U.S. personnel. While Pablo was in no way a saint, he needed the cooperation of these jungle residents to successfully develop his infrastructure. Pablo's boys only terminated American undercover agents and those who had worked with them, and they did so in an efficient manner. This infuriated the DEA officials into a campaign to smear Pablo's reputation, and turn his popularity into hatred.

The irony of all of this is summed up in one simple question – if you tell a lie and you're the only one believing it, then who is really being fooled? The Indians knew Pablo, and he provided them with the necessities of life that created a bond of loyalty. The more the U.S. tried to disgrace him, the more the people loved him. The United States propaganda machine and its associated press were the ones making Pablo bigger than life itself, and paved the way to the top for him.

I have to clarify this issue right now. Pablo was a businessman. That meant that my activities were a competition to him, even though I detested the cocaine trade and I was only ever involved with transporting marijuana. The cartels and Pablo wanted my airstrips to refuel their planes from Bolivia and Peru, and they wanted the plantations of my friends to grow coca plants. The Medellín Valley was the largest Cannabis Sativa belt in the Americas. It was 500 miles long and averaged about 75 miles wide. There were never any coca plants in Colombia before the late 70s.

When we arrived in Del Diablo there was a bonfire on the beach, and it was so large that we could see it from miles out at sea as we approached. It was time for a celebration and we were all greeted as if we were royalty. My presence alone indicated that there was going to be an economic boost for the tribe. It was like the arrival of Santa Claus at Christmastime, because my boat was loaded with a lot of needed dry goods, stores, blankets, and tools, plus even more medicines and hospital supplies. I felt like I was part of the Peace Corps at times like this. It was like living National Geographic magazine, not just reading it.

The Dudley's crew, along with Mark and Hal, all enjoyed the feast of roasted pig, smoked fish, lobster, crab, corn, snails and overproof bootleg rum. As they feasted, Larry and I went over the plans for loading the boats in the morning with the help of my "regulars." The locals had just met Larry for the first time, and they were intimidated by his size. Larry was about 6'5" and around 350 pounds, and his right hand was about the size of their heads. Still, it didn't take long for them to realize that I wouldn't have brought Larry along if I had any reservations about him, and my trust was good enough for them. Also, the use of both boats would clear the village of both loads that were "backed up." The

49

intention was to expedite the loading ASAP and get home. Pot warehoused in the village was a big danger to men, women and children, should the wrong people (like the DEA) discover it. They could all be executed and the village burned to the ground. The DEA does not take prisoners outside the U.S. They did not have a way to jail them, and dead men tell no tales. It was absolute termination – leave no witnesses. I still have nightmares to this day, and have since been diagnosed with Post Traumatic Stress Disorder. This is the first time that I have ever documented these events in fear of repercussion by U.S. authorities.

At dawn Alberto and I woke the crew to get the show on the road. We needed to load around 130,000 pounds that were in bales weighing between 55 and 80 pounds each. Considering that a cayuca can only safely carry a maximum of 20 bales at a time, it was going to take about 5 trips on each of the village's 20 cayucas to move the loads, paddling a round-trip distance of 7 miles on each trip. We needed to be organized, as there was no room for error.

The crew, however, was a complete mess. They were hung-over, sick and reluctant to leave. They evidently "went native" on us and had decided that life down here was an improvement over the civilized prisons we call cities in America. The natives were closer to the concept of Eden than the Anglo concept of world domination. It took me over an hour to talk some sense into them and remind them of our mission here. I finally had to promise them that after we made the delivery to the U.S. they could return to this place. I also informed them that the longer our boats were offshore, the more likely they could be spotted by DEA surveillance aircraft. That thought finally put the scare in them, shaking them into a return to reality. By noon we were loaded and ready to head north.

The current through the Yucatan Straits runs northward at about 3 knots. The trip to South America took approximately 7 days in my boat, but only 6 days to return home when I was able to surf the current back. I could gain about 75 miles a day if I paid attention to my navigation and rode the center of the main current. The only problem was the fact that the Dudley was a conventional fishing boat and not modified for speed. At best, she would only be able to make 200 miles per day, and there were 1500 miles between us and Louisiana, our destination. This was going to take about 8 days, with the Dudley following me in the Joe Louis.

We started seeing offshore oilrigs after 7 days at sea – this was a sign we were within 200 miles of the U.S. The bad news was that this meant we were in waters controlled by the Coast Guard, with so many oil rigs that we needed to remain alert on our radar so as to not run into any of them. The good news was that the congested waters provided electronic and visual protection, so we could use certain elements to our advantage.

I would always stagger my timing to enter a harbor around sunset. The sun's position on the horizon creates a glare to those facing the west, and those facing the east have a background that is darker with the glass of the boat creating reflections that break up her profile like camouflage. It makes indefinable silhouettes that can't be accurately described to authorities.

We entered the jetty at Holly Beach, Louisiana at around 7:30pm, giving us enough time to cruise up the Calcasieu River slowly and quietly until we arrived at Hackberry Landing at about 9pm. That was perfect, since it was dark and we could unload both boats before midnight and be outside the channel on the ocean before dawn. If we came under suspicion then, it wouldn't matter – the trucks would already be long gone and on the way to their destinations.

While unloading, I was greeted by David, who handled all of my U.S. intelligence and monitored every bit of information that was beneficial to my activities. I prefer to take calculated risks. We may have appeared to be a bunch of high seas smugglers, but the truth of the matter is that we had degrees in fields like Physics, Mathematics, Electronic Sciences and Engineering. Every move we made was dictated by the results of crunching numbers against Theory and Probability. To be more accurate, chaos theory and Murphy's Law were more the governing rule. But, this time, David delivered some information that we hadn't predicted, and it was terrifying news. I had purchased the Joe Louis from some Cubans in Miami for $20,000 U.S., and David revealed that the reason I had gotten such a good deal on her was because she was on an Interpol hotsheet for gun-running in and out of Cuba. Everyone was looking for her. It is common practice for the Coast Guard to blast gun-runners out of the water, long before there is an opportunity to enter into an engagement or, as it's better known, a fire-fight.

I knew I had to get rid of the boat, and that I had to do it right away. It was devastating to me, because I felt a bond with her based on all that we had been through together over the past few weeks. She had served me well.

Then I remembered. At the mouth of the inlet, where we had come in, there was a Coast Guard station at Monkey Island. It was a holding yard for boats that had been impounded for smuggling. There was a lot of activity there, as it was also a fuel depot that serviced oil supply vessels and fishing fleets 24 hours a day.

I told Eileen to drive our pickup truck to the ferry landing at Holly Beach and wait for me there with a fresh set of clothes. I then boarded the Joe Louis and headed for Monkey Island. Having already cleared the boat of anything valuable and having destroyed my logbook, I timed my entry into the basin with a couple other fishing boats that were fueling up. It was too easy. I pulled off and headed into the impound area wearing my wetsuit. I gingerly slid up to another boat that was impounded, shut her down, tied her off and said a final goodbye. With one last affectionate twist of the main spoke of her wheel, I left the pilothouse, put on my swim fins, mask and snorkel, and then quietly slid over the side. I swam with the current past the fuel dock and grabbed a tire hanging over the side of a tugboat that was heading out. The tugboat towed me out of the harbor and down the Calcasieu River towards Holly Beach and Eileen.

As we neared the ferry landing, I released my hold on the tire and swam to the wharf. Eileen was there with my clothes and our two Doberman Pinschers Affy and Gypsy. I was safe, and there were no loose ends. The feds wouldn't find the Joe Louis, as they would never look in their own backyard. And that is exactly what happened. They didn't discover her there until 1980, and only when I informed them of her whereabouts. I can't tell you how embarrassed they were, but I can say this – they hate me to this very day.

1976 – The Aquarian Sea

Eileen and the dogs and I next moved to California. I acquired a 150 foot all steel shrimp boat named the Aquarian Sea. She was located in Aransas Pass, Texas. This was a pretty good deal, as she also had a berth at a commercial dock and was well known in the area. There would not be too many questions or harbor talk about the deal. The "good ole' boys" like to keep things in a private sort of way, and those who couldn't understand the rules seemed to just disappear without any questions. We were still near bayou country and it was good for business. In fact we were not far from Whiskey Bay, a place my uncles used to talk about during their Prohibition stories of "back in the day."

The Aquarian Sea was quite a step up for us. She had full climate control with central heat and air conditioning. She had watertight doors, all electric galley, private crew quarters, Captain's quarters, twin diesel engines, twin generators, walk in refrigerator, walk in freezer, full shower and 3 heads (toilets). We could carry 10,000 gallons of fresh water, and 60,000 gallons of fuel, which gave us an endurance at sea for at least 120 days or 31,000 nautical miles. We had Full Ocean's capability. Her fish hold could accommodate 120,000 pounds of pot or the equivalent of six refrigerated tractor-trailer rigs.

To maintain a normal appearance we made several trips with her as a shrimp boat during the lull between trips for weed. We used to laugh when we saw other fish boats coming in buried to their water line and there were no seagulls harassing them. It was a dead giveaway that they were not loaded with fish or shrimp. This is why when we came in we would throw our nets at the 200 mile limit, cover the deck with fish and shrimp, and then shovel them into our wake. The birds would go nuts, and everything appeared normal.

We went down to the Rosalind Bank and were shrimping when on our second day we hit a school of super jumbo shrimp. They were almost the size of rock lobster. We chased that school for two days and filled our holds. When we came into Port Arthur, Texas the fish house called National Fisherman Magazine and broke the story. This was good for us as it kept our cover story as shrimpers. The shrimp were super jumbo prawns and we made a lot of money. This was really a wild stroke of luck – or so we thought.

A week later I got a call to go to New Orleans and arrange another run down to the "Lions Paw" at the "Five Fingers." We left around 10pm on a Wednesday night. We were all tripping on chocolate mescaline, and no one could stop laughing. Though the crew was stoned out, they were more than capable. This was no more than an extension of our daily duties, which we did all the time smoking pot.

I cast off from the dock and we headed out into the channel at low tide. We would ride out with the tide and be long gone by sun up. After a while I noticed that we hadn't cleared the channel marker. I checked the radar and we weren't really coming up on the next marker. I left the pilothouse and looked over the stern, we had a wake, but when I looked over the side it didn't look like we were moving. I went up to the bow expecting to see the bone in her teeth (white water from her pushing through the water). There was no bone. We weren't moving. I asked "C.K." what color the next marker light was. If it was red or green that would tell me where I was in the channel. His reply was purple! For the last 2 hours we had been stuck on a mud bank, as the wet Texas mud and water looked identical on a moonless night. I was laughing so hard I could hardly climb back into the captain's chair. I put her in reverse, changed course 30 degrees and got back into the center of the channel. By sunrise we were out on open sea headed for the Yucatan Straits.

The next evening after sunset I started radar plotting to find a safe course through all of the oil rigs. There were so many of them in the gulf that you could easily run into one if its lights were out. Some of the old wells were no more than a pipe sticking up out of the water. Long ago abandoned, these wells did not have an oil rig to mark them. A lot of boats ran into these and went quickly to the bottom. After all, a collision at sea can ruin your whole day.

Soon I noticed that we were being followed by a lot of fishing boats. I guess they decided to follow us to where those jumbo shrimp were at. I opened up the throttles and we started pulling away, but a few of them were still keeping up. I changed our course to the east and headed towards the Virgin Islands. I called the crew to quarters and we had a meeting as to what we were going to do. We had no other choice. We were getting out of the fish business that night and become an oil supply
54

boat for the Gulf of Mexico. You should have seen the look on their faces. They were sure that this plan was spawned from the mescaline – and it probably was.

After dark that night we fired up all our deck lights. We dropped our nets in the water and started shrimping. I was sure that the other boats would do the same. This put a full load on our outriggers and our tower. Earlier that day I had the crew transfer all of our antennas and electronics to the roof of the pilothouse. At about midnight we fired up the cutting torches and I cut the welds on the Marco winches. We cut through the supports for the tower and the outriggers – but not all the way. When that was done I went forward and set up the torches in the bow near the anchor winch. I had the crew go inside and C.K. pushed the throttles wide open. I crouched down in the gunwales above the forecastle, and reached up with the torch - cutting through the shackle on the forward guy wires. It tore open like a gunshot! Cables went flying through the air. The outriggers swept back, and the tower followed after them while dragging the Marco winches in tow. It was spectacular! Equipment was flying everywhere - and in a few seconds it was all over. A quarter of a million dollars worth of fishing gear was dragged astern, overboard and headed for Davy Jones' Locker in about 1,200 fathoms of water! One minute our boat had been a large bright radar blip, the next minute we were gone. I ran into the pilothouse, shut off all our lights, brought her around 180 degrees to starboard, and set a new course for the Yucatan.

We were now an oil supply vessel. The next morning was spent cleaning up the mess, cutting off mounting tabs, tossing the remainder of the fish gear over-board and re-painting the steel from the burn marks. Later that night I confirmed that the plan had worked, as we had lost our tail of fishing boats. I radioed Fred and had him "arrange" the paperwork for me, transferring the Aquarian Sea from a fish boat to a registered commercial oil supply vessel.

Nine days later we were off the Lions Paw at The Five Fingers in Colombian waters. We loaded in record time and within 48 hours we were headed back to Louisiana.

At dawn a twin engine Piper buzzed us. I knew the plane, and it was Alberto Weber. He was crazier than me, and flew a plane like I handled a boat. His father had been a U-Boat Kapitan who defected with his crew during World War II, scuttling the sub in the Caribbean. He took asylum in Colombia for the rest of the war, married and raised a family. This was more common than some people think. Not all of the Wehrmacht agreed with Hitler, but the U-Boat captains could do something about it. They headed to South America and abandoned their boats. There are scuttled U-Boats all over the Caribbean.

Anyway, Alberto was now flying right toward my pilothouse windows no more than 50 feet above the water! Right when I thought he was going to hit us he pulled straight up and a yellow package was thrown from the plane. It was a life jacket. C.K. went over the side and grabbed it as I brought the Aquarian Sea to a halt. When we had C.K. back on board I found a map of Portland Maine Harbor in a plastic bag. When I opened the chart there was a red circle drawn around a dock in the harbor with a time and a date.

C.K. was a good first mate that I had acquired from the Texas Boys in Aransas. He was all Texan, complete with cowboy boots chewing tobacco and a Texas drawl. Not the sharpest tool in the shed, but he knew how to take orders and how to give them. The crew respected him and that was very important in my absence. He lived on the Aquarian Sea, literally, and took care of her as if he was the owner. That boy was pure Texas pride, and I knew the boat was in good hands when I was not around between trips.

As it turned out our disappearing act was the talk of Port Arthur and all through the Sabine Pass. All of the fishermen that had been following us were talking it up in port about us dropping out of sight while fishing. There were even some stories about UFO abduction from some of the Jack Daniels for lunch bunch. At any rate we were the talk of the fishing community there, and we couldn't go back now with a load of marijuana, and expect to covertly unload it without drawing a lot of attention. Everyone would be looking for us. They had a lot of questions and we had a lot of explaining to do.

My counterintelligence director, David, and I had a contingency plan with alternate landing places in the event that the political atmosphere changed while we were out at sea. It was designed for this kind of situation. But Portland Maine! It was December. We were wearing Hawaiian shirts, shorts and sandals! We were equipped with enough stores and fuel for the trip, but my charts stopped at the Mona Passage in the Virgin Islands. I would have to dead recon some 3,500 miles of

North Atlantic Ocean during the worst time of year before we came onto the chart they had given us. It was our only option now, and we had to rise to the occasion.

I changed our course to head for the Mona Passage and called the crew to the galley to inform them of the situation. To my surprise they took it very well. While we were short on warm clothing, we did have survival suits, wet suits and central heating. We had more than enough fuel and enough food to last a couple of months.

I cleared off the galley table and put the chart for Portland on one end and the chart for Mona Passage on the other end. In those days we navigated using Loran C which worked off of 37 beacons worldwide that generated a signal. By its intensity and its crossing over another signal a navigator could plot his position within an accuracy of 2 miles or less during the day. At night with a full moon (due to propagation) our accuracy could be within a 1/10 mile. I located two signals on each chart that were the same and now we had a link to the charts. Using the latitude and longitude lines and a pair of dividers I was able to space the charts apart with precision. I taped the charts to the edges of the table and for the next two days I kept extending the loran signal curves until their arcs coincided with the charts. With a calculator I assigned the signal strengths to the arcs. These arcs were drawn on the white Formica galley tabletop and I blatantly – in no uncertain terms - declared the galley table off limits, as it was now a navigation station. If those marks were smeared or lost I could not re-assign them as we had already passed our given reference points and we were technically in no man's land.

The Bowditch Sea Mounts are northwest of Bermuda Island in the Atlantic. They were like fissures or stalagmites on the ocean floor which would have become islands had they made it to the surface thousands of years before during the volcanic activity that formed Bermuda.

As we were heading north just outside of the Eastern Ridge of the Bahamas, the appearance of the Bowditch Sea Mounts on our fathometer would confirm the accuracy of my time and distance calculations and current drift estimate. Their peaks would be obvious spikes on my fathometer, which not only gave a visual display, but also produced a paper graph. We were navigating by deduced reckoning, but I also held a few aces in my hand by utilizing everything I had in creative ways.

The weather bulletins were depressing and our barometer was bottoming out. There was a severe low atmospheric pressure drop. A hurricane was forming and the weather service had named her Clara. She formed and hit within 24 hours. We were heading right into the eye of the storm. We could not alter our course or speed, because it would alter all my calculations. So we buckled down for worse. The first 24 hours were the worst as we were in the outer ring. The wind velocity was a consistent 80 mph with occasional gusts to 150+. That is all the wind speed indicator was scaled for. The waves were over 40 feet and the tops were being blown off of them like the foam on a beer. It was like being on a rollercoaster ride at an amusement park ride.

After about 30 hours we entered into the center, or eye, of Clara. It is hard to explain how strange it is in there with no horizon. The sea was flat and no winds, you could not see the sun, but the sky was amber and reflected off of the glassy flat sea. That is why you could not discern the horizon, as the sky just flowed into the ocean, without a contrast line to separate them. It was a rare spectacular sight to see, and I know that the crew probably talks about it to this day. To our advantage Clara was heading north along a path that was close to our course. We would be able to enjoy the phenomenon for a while.

As with all things wonderful they were soon to end. About two days later Clara decided to head for Open Ocean to the east. We were now going to have to fight our way out of her. Her wrath had increased, and she was to deal with us as a scorned woman. For a while, we had intimately resided within her, and she would be vindictive about our departure. She had provided us with exactly what we had needed. Our path through the Mona Passage had been concealed visually and electronically, as if it never happened.

We were about to endure 3 days and nights of severe weather and rain that ran horizontal and acted like a sand blaster. It removed some of our paint, all of our deck gear and even some of our antenna and weather equipment. During this time we could overhear radio transmissions from a vessel sending a Mayday to Whiskey Oscar Mike, the Coast Guard base in Miami. She was a 50-foot sailboat with a family on board that had moderate sailing experience. They were being severely beaten by Clara and taking on water. The Coast Guard informed them that the weather and sea conditions prevented them from deploying rescue vessels.

After an hour of this air traffic I became so angry that I picked up the mic and told off the Coast Guard for their cowardice. I have always had a problem keeping my mouth shut, and they wanted to know who we were. I did not respond. Instead I contacted the skipper of the sailboat on channel 16 and we located his position with our radio direction finder, or R.D.F. We were heading in his direction and with a minor course change we could intercept him. We took turns talking to him, his crew and his family to keep them calm, but most of all to lock in their position with the R.D.F. This was vital as visual conditions were poor from the storm and radar blips would flicker in and out as the boat would be high on a wave and then buried in the swell. They would be like trying to find a needle in a haystack.

We located him about 9 hours later. I had the crew put the inflatable dingy over the side to get them off their boat and on to ours. I put 3 of my boys on their boat in order to assess the damage and to pump the water out of their boat and to make any necessary repairs. This family thought we were angels or something. They were so grateful. Everett, our cook (or should I say chef), made them all hot soup and the crew donated dry towels and clothes. We washed and dried their clothes with our washer and dryer. As my crew completed repairs on their boat I instructed them not to leave the salon for any reason and we would do all we could to assist them.

By the middle of the day we had their sailboat seaworthy again. It was difficult to explain why we needed them to leave the safety of our larger boat, but I reassured them that as Clara was passing out to sea things would be calming down. They wanted to know who we were so that they could thank us. I blatantly told them that if they were truly grateful they would never – ever mention us or our acts of generosity. I explained that it was in the best interest of both parties to forget about us as we did not exist, we were ghosts like the "Flying Dutchmen." I used their charts to confirm our position and set a new course for Portland. We were just off the Georgia coast about 800 miles into the Atlantic when we said goodbye. I had given them a course of 240-degree west, which would put them between Daytona Beach and Miami in about four days. We all felt pretty good about ourselves, and the irony of all this is that smugglers are often depicted as pirates whereas nothing could be further from the truth – at least in our case. We took the risk of discovery and liability to assist an American family in peril when their own government agency denied them.

Two days later we caught a spike on our fathometer. It was the Bowditch Sea Mounts, also known as the Pinnacles. Their name came from a master mariner and navigator by the name of Nathaniel Bowditch. He discovered them while establishing the timetables, celestial almanac, current charts and prevailing wind charts for the McKay Shipping Company, operators of the famed McKay Clipper Ships. Their Atlantic crossings were the most consistent, predictable, and efficient means of cargo and passenger travel between the U.S. and Europe during the 1800's giving them the nickname "the Greyhounds of the Sea" after the racing dog of that breed.

This gave me an accurate indication of where we were, which was about 50 miles west of Bermuda. We could swing our course around 10 degrees to the west so as to cut paper on our Portland chart in a little over four days. To be perfectly honest here, I must admit that I was extremely nervous as to whether my bright idea would work. When I first came up with this plan I was confident, and that helped reassure the crew that they were in competent hands. But in a couple of days the facts would speak for themselves. The crew had started a pool as to when – time and date – we would cut paper on the Portland chart. This was good therapy for them, but it added extra stress to my situation. If I was wrong a panic would spread through the boat quickly. We were in unfamiliar waters, with over 100,000 pounds of marijuana onboard with no contingency plan for escape. In fact, this was already the contingency plan, right? I had never failed them before.

I started to scrutinize every aspect in the legend on the chart. That is when I saw it! My heart sunk – how could this be possible? Most charts have a variation and deviation chart on the compass rose. This is to compensate for anomalies of magnetic fields in the earth vs. true north. They are usually 3 or 4 degrees east or west depending on where you were in the world. Here I am, looking at a deviation in excess of 28 degrees! That is when I discovered a warning in small red letters. I was near an uninhabited island that was made of pure lodestone or magnetic iron ore. I could only wonder how the local mariners could deal with this, especially in a fog. I wondered what other surprises would be in store for us.

We came in to the Portland Maine chart at six in the morning. I confirmed this with a 3 way Loran position and the triangle was smaller than a pinhead. This confirmed our position to less than 1/10 mile of accuracy. I was smiling from ear to ear, but said nothing. I just marked it on the chart on the galley table and waited for the crew to make comments. I was struggling to hide my excitement; I wanted to brag about it. I decided I could have more fun letting them talk it up for awhile, while I displayed the image of a competent mariner and navigator extraordinaire.

We had traveled over 5,000 miles from Sabine Pass, to Colombia South America, to the Mona Passage, to Portland Maine. Almost 2,000 miles of the trip was by the seat of our pants. As far as I am concerned this feat rivaled Captain Bligh's journey when he was set adrift by Fletcher Christian when the crew of the Bounty mutinied. Anyway, that's my story and I'm stickin' to it.

The fact of the matter is that we cut paper about four hours earlier than I predicted and we were less than 100 miles east of my estimation. If you consider the rescue, the flow of the gulf stream, and Clara, I would say we had done quite remarkably well.

Portland, Maine

We still had to enter the harbor, find the pier, and unload the cargo. We used our radar to navigate the harbor, as it gave us a view that was identical to the chart. The pier was an old fishing dock covered with many fish houses. It had been the center of the industry back in the day, but it was somewhat worn for wear and run down by then. Fred and some others met us who had spotted us from the air the day before. We never used radios when we had a load on board. It just wasn't done for many reasons, the worst being the ill chance of being triangulated by the Coast Guard.

Smugglers had to be independently self sufficient, silent, and unquestionably accountable for their own safety, and unequally proficient at their tasks. Calling for help was completely out of the question. It was not only an invitation to a prison sentence, but even worse, the possibility of being shot right out of the water.

We tied up to the fish dock, and the truck was being brought in when Mac showed up in a panic. Mac was part of Dave's counter intelligence group and he ran down to warn us that the cops were on their way. We already had bales of marijuana all over the deck waiting for the conveyors. We shut the cargo hold, covered the bales with tarps and C.K. ran up to the wheelhouse. The engine room crew locked all the hatches and began making preparations to run for open water. They were ready to activate "Evacuation Order 86", which is to run for open water and scuttle the boat.

I was wearing 5 t-shirts of different colors because of the cold. Mac said that his scanner confirmed that I had been spotted. I took off running down the pier between fish houses, nets, fish boxes and equipment. At each interval of rest I peeled off a t-shirt and became a new color. As I tried to circle back to the boat from the shadows an arm reached out and grabbed me. My heart stopped. I was caught! Not by the police - but by one of our contacts at the landing spot. He gave me a jacket and told me to follow him quickly. We walked back down the pier, and up some steps to an office. Fred was there; Danny and Ray were also there. Boy was I glad to see them. They told me to put on some foul weather gear to hide my shorts and not a moment too soon. A minute later there was a knock on the door, and a couple of Portland Police officers were asking if they had seen someone running around in a yellow t-shirt. Our contacts said no, but that they would call if they did. It turns out that our local contacts knew these cops as it was part of their patrol or beat for years. The cops said that they had spotted a couple of stolen cars nearby and when a strange boat showed up from Texas they thought they could be related. Soon they left after having a couple of drinks, and we resumed our work.

When we returned to the boat, Mike, my Chief Engineer, did not want to unlock the hatch and come out. He had already put fuses in the explosives in the event that he needed to scuttle the boat. He made that decision when they looked out the ventilator on the after deck to see cops crawling and stumbling and cussing all over the marijuana that was under the tarps. The police never saw the bales, and they soon left.

We had lost precious time, and there were only a few hours left before sun up. We got busy fast, and loaded five forty foot trucks in less than three hours, a new record. I figure that it was due to the adrenaline running through our veins. As the sun came up I gave C.K. and the crew about $120,000 in cash and told them to take the Aquarian Sea to Boston, refuel and head back to Texas. I would meet up with them in San Francisco in the middle of January to pay them. As they left for open sea I could finally relax. Ray and Dan put me in this limo to take me to the airport. There was a Hansa jet there that supposedly all of us owned, so to speak, and the pilot was instructed to fly me wherever I needed to go. They would fly a commercial carrier to Detroit, meet the trucks, and finish the job. My end of the deal was completed.

So there I was at the airport, no baggage, no sleep in 3 days, no bath in a week, no coat, just a Hawaiian shirt, shorts, sandals, long hair and I was covered in a brownish green dust from the pot. The limo driver was escorting me through the airport to the private lounge used for corporate jets. There were these beautiful women on the arms of captains of industry dressed in thousand dollar outfits and Italian suits, and there I was... a mess. They snubbed me immediately with a look of question as to what I was doing there. The limo driver procured for me a bottle of *Cabernet Sauvignon,* and we sat looking out the window at the runway. Then the Hansa showed up, and all of these suits are admiring it, and commenting about it. The pilots exited the jet and walked towards the stairway that led up to the lounge where we were and came in. They approached me and asked, "Captain Duke, are you ready?"

I said, "Yes," turned to the astonished people, raised my glass to them in a toast, swallowed the rest, set the glass on the bar, put the bottle under my arm, and left with the pilots to board the plane.

The Hansa was a German built equivalent of what a Lear Jet was back in the 1970's. They were much faster, but they did not have as much range. To fly to San Francisco we would need to refuel in Denver, Colorado. No problem, I needed the sleep anyway, so I rolled up a fat joint from some fresh Thai stick, smeared the paper with honey oil, and poured another glass of wine. I figured I deserved it after the last few weeks; after all I had just delivered 60 million dollars worth of marijuana - and that was at *wholesale prices*. My crew would split 6 million dollars. Not bad for a months work.

Hansa jet photo copyright Eduard Marmet – Airliners.net

1978 - The DAKOTA DC3

In late 1977 the political climate was becoming unstable in Colombia, South America. Cocaine was taking over the U.S. markets, and smugglers from all over were trying to access our areas of the Medellín Valley to refuel the airplanes headed for America. The U.S. Black Op teams of the D.E.A. were murdering complete villages trying to take control of the drug trade. These mercenaries were the most ruthless humans I ever encountered. Whenever one of their own was seriously wounded they would just shoot him in the head, remove all his clothes and anything (including cutting off tattoos) to hide the fact that there were American operatives down there.

They had a scapegoat by the name of Pablo Escobar. He was a hero to most of the remote villagers, but I did not particularly like him. You see, he needed our areas to refuel his planes. The planes were coming out of Bolivia and/or Peru, and did not have the range to make it all the way to the United States. By refueling in our area it would increase their options for landing sites. I could not trust anyone in the cocaine trade. They always carried guns, they were unreliable and most of the time they were under the influence of their product, cocaine.

At first we didn't mind them landing and buying fuel. We enjoyed snorting a few lines and drinking Triete - an over proof rum in a 3 sided bottle. After a while, though, it seemed like once they got their foot in the door we couldn't get rid of them. It was obvious that they were drawing a lot of heat from the D.E.A. If Pablo and the D.E.A. wanted to go to war, fine, who were we to try and stop it? We were smugglers, not mercenaries. We carried guns, but rarely had to use them. It just wasn't right to be in mortal combat around marijuana. It was a contradiction in terms as marijuana was a propitiator, which enlightened one to a higher respect for life. We were compelled *not* to kill, or engage in acts of violence. Not everyone shared our opinion.

After the Portland adventure I decided to buy an airplane. This would speed up the process of getting the bales out of the Medellín Valley and down the coast. In "Trade-A-Plane" I found a DC3 for sale in Fort Lauderdale, Florida, for $25,000. Ray and I went down, looked at it, and

I fell in love with it. It was completely rebuilt with 0 hours SMOH (since major over haul). The company who did the work just wanted their money as the original owners had disappeared a year ago. They "lien-sold" it and I bought it. The cockpit just sang with "Boogie Woogie Blues" from World War II. It was also easy to convert to hauling cargo, as in less than an hour two men could remove all of the seats.

Dakota DC -3 airplane photo by Nicholas Rjabow – Bigstockphoto.com

She had a pair of Pratt-Whitney twin wasp 1,200 hp radial engines, and had been modified from the original two blade propellers to three blade constant speed propellers. The engines were turbocharged. This gave her an advantage for short takeoff while fully loaded. We could squeeze about 12,000 pounds of baled marijuana in her and still get the door shut. She had an overhead window up in the cockpit for navigation and that could be opened for an access hatch. When fully loaded that was the only way in and out. She carried enough fuel to give us a cruising time of around 10 hours at a little over 230 mph, giving us a cruising range of nearly 2,200 miles.

As a kid at Put-in-Bay I spent a lot of time in the winter flying around in some old Ford Tri-Motors. These were three engine aircraft built by Henry Ford after he bailed Bill Stout (of Stout Metal Aircraft) out of

68

bankruptcy in the late 20's. They were the backbone of TWA until the introduction of the DC3. These planes served as our supply link to the mainland between the times when Lake Erie was navigable by boat, and when the lake would freeze solid enough to drive on. They carried the mail, students, supplies and even a coffin or two if needed. I used to ride in the co-pilot seat as often as possible when they were hauling freight. Old Harold Hauch and Nuell Whittey were the pilots, and I took advantage of every opportunity to fly with them. They wouldn't let me take off or land the planes, but they did let me fly them, and set up approaches to land. I was learning to fly on instruments, as I was too short to see out the windscreen. By the time I was 20 years old I probably had about 100 or more hours as a co-pilot. They taught me how to do pre-flight inspections and flight checklists and the basic care and handling of aircraft. They emphasized the importance of these, as you cannot fix things in the air. That is where I learned my 5 P's: Prior Planning Prevents Poor Performance!

I called Mike, my Chief Engineer, one day and had him fly to Fort Lauderdale. I picked him up at the airport in a rented car and we drove to an old airfield a few miles from Miami International Airport.

I showed him the DC3 and he looked a little puzzled. We went over and opened the passenger-boarding door and went in. Within a few minutes he felt the presence of the 1940's era and said that all this plane needed was some nose art. He was still curious as to what it was we were doing with this airplane. I closed the boarding door and we walked forward up to the cockpit. I sat in the pilot's seat on the left and told him to sit in the co-pilot's seat to my right and to buckle up. I wish I had a picture of the expression on Mike's face.

I primed the engines after calling off the checklist. I yelled, "clear" out the window and started cranking over the port engine. She lit. I told Mike to yell, "clear" out his window, and then fired the starboard engine and she lit. I called the tower and we were cleared for takeoff. We taxied over to the runway, set the brakes and ran the radials up to the red line. I gave her about 25% flaps and let the brakes off. As we gained speed I kept cranking on more pitch to the propellers keeping the engines below the red line. In a couple of hundred feet we were off the ground and heading east for the Bahamas.

Mike said, "I didn't know you had a pilot's license."

I replied, "I don't, but we made it this far." You should have seen the look on his face. Then I told him that I knew how to fly, but I just never took the time to register and get my license. Well, as Mike would be, he asked what we were going to do when we land and someone starts asking questions. I reassured him that nobody will ask us any questions when we land in El Banco, Colombia. I think that if Mike had a parachute he would have jumped. He was not real happy about being shanghaied, but isn't that what friends are all about?

Alberto was going to meet us in El Banco and would fly us back to Texas after dark in his Piper. I started a crash course on flying for Mike, and in a few minutes I had him on the yoke. He was a natural. He watched his gauges, altimeter, turn and bank indicator, and bubble horizon. As with many first time fliers he would drop altitude from trying to see the horizon. He was doing so well I rolled up a big fat Thai stick with, of course, honey oil, and 4 1/2 hours later we were off the coast of Colombia passing Santa Marta, then passed Cienaga and on into the interior heading for El Banco at the north end of the Medellín Valley. I really think that Mike actually enjoyed flying that old plane, and I am sure that this is one of his favorite stories to this day.

I had met Mike at Ray's house in Belvedere, Ca. two years earlier. He was my age and about the same height standing 5'-7" tall. He was a gifted mechanic, and machinist, that had a passion for old school designs, and equipment. He was meticulously clean, and orderly, and maintained his work area, tools and equipment cleaner than the kitchens of most fine restaurants. Technically Mike was my equal in rank as far as the engine-room was concerned. He was the number-one officer below deck, and I was careful to accord him all of the respect due to his position of authority. He and I were mutually dependent upon each other for safe and efficient operation of the vessel. There were often times of disagreement between us, but it was never displayed or verbalized in the vicinity of the crew.

When we landed Alberto was already there. He was really impressed with the plane, and immediately named it "DAKOTA," a nick-name for the aircraft from World War II. Alberto was twin engine certified and was an extraordinary pilot in every aspect of the term. He had an aerobatics license, and spent hours flying his Hans Christian Eagle in altitudes that just baffled my comprehension of flight. We once flew

70

from El Banco to Cienaga doing rolls all the way there. When we landed I could not walk. I got out of the plane, fell on the ground, and tossed my lunch. I may not have been doing rolls anymore, but my brain was.

After about an hour of inspecting and drooling over our new acquisition we climbed into the Piper and took off for an old airstrip near Port Arthur, Texas. As usual, when we were 3 miles off the coast of Columbia in an area called Turbo, Alberto dropped to sea level. We were flying so low that I was afraid of running into a sailboat, or a container ship coming out of Panama.

1978 - The POLAR SEA

When we finally got back to the West Coast I made arrangements to go to Seattle, Washington. In the "Boat and Harbors" trade paper I had found a Miki tugboat for sale. She was 140 feet long, and had majestic classic lines of an era gone by. She was the epitome of wooden boat construction launched in 1944. Her formal number was U.S. Army LT 141. This ocean going tugboat was one of sixty-one built during World War II, and had a low radar signature. It also had incredible towing capabilities in any weather that the Gulf of Alaska or the Bering Straits could conjure up. They would haul barges full of supplies and cargo on the Pineapple routes between the U.S. and Hawaii. They also ran between Long Beach and Dutch Harbor Alaska delivering equipment and supplies for the construction of the Alcan Highway. The first of these tugs was constructed in 1941, but the boat I was looking at was one of the last ones built, and therefore was the best of the construction. Her name was The Polar Sea, and she was available at a reasonable price, $125,000 cash.

The POLAR SEA

The Polar Sea was powered by a direct-reversible Superior VDMSS inline or straight 8. This engine was over 14 feet tall, and more than 24 feet long. She idled at 32 RPM and maxed out at 425 RPM. We could cruise her at about 350-375 RPM for months at a time without too much harmonic distortion. The engine needed an engineering crew to oil her valve train manually, to regulate her temperature by increasing or decreasing the water flow through her heat exchangers, and monitor all of her vitals. That was because there were no automated systems incorporated into the design.

We upgraded her by balancing her crankshaft and flywheel, which weighed around 93,000 pounds. This was an extremely delicate task, as we had to dismantle the engine, lean the main block over to one side, and remove the crankshaft-flywheel assembly through the opening where we had removed her exhaust stack. While the yard crane was doing the lift I was so tense that you could not have shoved a hypodermic needle up my ass with a jack-hammer. If the lift cables snapped or slipped, a 93,000 pound lawn-dart would have ripped through the hull. That would have been the end of the Polar Sea. While that was underway I found a turbocharger off an LST main engine that I could adapt to our Superior Diesel increasing her from 1,500 BHP to over 2,500 BHP. I also located a four-blade propeller that was 10 feet in diameter and had 60 inches of pitch. That would give us a speed of 16-18 knots, which was a vast improvement over her registered speed of 10 knots. We could leave New Orleans and head for Puerto Rico, check in at Customs and file for a return to New Orleans at 10 knots; detour to Colombia, pick up a load, run it into Hackberry, Louisiana, unload, and still make it to New Orleans without being overdue on our estimated time of arrival, or anyone missing us.

With Alberto flying our load to the coast from the Medellín Valley we eliminated the donkey train, three weeks of jungle transport, shootouts, paramilitary engagements and exposure. This worked like a precision timepiece. It streamlined our operation with financial benefits from less overhead and loss, but most of all from bandits, Colombian *Federales*, or D.E.A. Black Ops.

In 1977 the D.E.A. offered Colombian fishermen and locals a reward for any American smugglers captured. The reward was $10,000 per person and the surrender of the American vessels, which they could keep. This was a lucrative proposition for coastal Colombians whose annual salary was half of the bounty for just one person, or $5,000 U.S. dollars a year.

Coming out of Cienaga one afternoon we spotted a strange formation of fishing boats on the radar. It looked like it was trying to form a circle around us. I grabbed the binoculars and noticed that these boats were dragging their fishnets on the surface of the water several hundred feet behind them. I was thinking how stupid that was as a boat near them could get her propeller caught in them. That's when the light went off in my head. This was not careless stupidity - this was intended!

The circle was not complete so I pushed the ships telegraph to full power and Mike called up from the engine room. He wanted to know what was up, and I told him that we needed all the power he could produce. The crew went to general quarters, battening down hatches, grabbing their firearms and clearing their "30cals." They started opening up with some serious firepower on the smaller, faster boats that were closing in on us.

The Colombians liked to fish with dynamite. Today they were fishing for us. They started throwing sticks at us, and they were getting too close. The explosions were shaking us so hard that a 4-inch oil line broke in the engine room. Mike called up to me and said he would have to shut her down. I told him if he did that we would all be kicking his ass in a Colombian prison or ridin' this bitch to the bottom. He got the point and said he could bypass our lubricating oil refiner for a short period of time and would start repairs immediately.

By then I was taking some serious evasive actions in the pilothouse. Bullets were ripping through radios, chart drawers, and cabin walls. Everywhere I could hear them whiz by like bees. That was when I noticed that Donald Duck's head was shot off. It was a float toy my crew had given me as a present, after one of my tyrannical lectures about completing menial tasks. At that point I became really angry, and when I stood up from sitting on the floor of the pilothouse, I saw a fishing boat a few hundred feet in front of me.

I aimed the bow of the Polar Sea right for her cabin doors and laid on the air horns. Within a few minutes there was a tremendous crash as we tore through that old fishing trawler like a knife through butter. I could see the Captain's eyes as big as baseballs as he dove over the side. Mike called up from the engine room, as they had all been thrown to the deck plates, and wondered what the fuck happened. I told him what had occurred and that the worst was over. We headed for Deep Ocean leaving a trail of debris and human carnage in our wake. The crew really pulled together as a team that day. Mike's boys below repaired the broken oil line in about 45 minutes, a job that normally would have taken 3 hours. We lost some paint off of the bow and our rubber push pad was seriously shifted by some sheared off shackles, but we were free and none of our crew even got a scratch. This was just another experience that would remind us of the reciprocity of our occupation. It would cost 10,000 dollars to fill all the bullet holes, and 20,000 dollars "hush" money to get it done at the Todd Ship Yard in Hackberry on the Calcasieu River when we reached home.

November, 1978 - Orange Sunrise

We departed New Orleans with the Polar Sea and headed for Aruba, an island off of the Venezuelan coast. The tug fit right in there, as it was a commercial port and also a tourist paradise. I could leave C.K., Mike, and the crew there with the boat and contact them when it was time to head to the coast at Del Diablo to load.

Alberto picked me up in the Piper, and we flew to Aguachica, where the DC3 was being kept and the crews were baling the trimmed pot. To bale the buds we put plastic bags in a trash compactor and shoveled the buds in to compress them. Some were rectangular and some were like cylinders, depending on the type of compactors used. This usually took a couple of days, and we would then start loading the "Dakota" (DC3) with bales to fly them to Riohacha (near Del Diablo) and stockpile the load for the Polar Sea to pick up in a couple of days.

On the morning of the second day I woke early to the sound of a thunder in the valley. The sun was just coming up but the animals were silent. There was a rumble coming from the south like a heard of stampeding buffalo. What in hell was that?

In a few seconds I could see the sky was thick with airplanes. I grabbed my binoculars and could barely believe my own eyes. American C-130's and C-140's were flying low and in numbers that were uncountable. An orange plume followed behind them much like crop dusters. As the first ones passed over we were covered with an orange sticky powder. It was everywhere. Alberto and I had run under the wing of the "Dakota" and avoided the worst of it. The workers and villagers were not so lucky. We could hear the sound of a second wave approaching. Alberto and I looked at each other and without a word we instinctively crawled up on the wing of the "Dakota" and climbed in through the roof hatch.

Without a pre-flight inspection or checklist, our hands clambered for primers and switches. We lit her off and started rolling out to the airstrip. Visibility was almost 0 as the windscreen and everything was covered with this orange stuff. We put our nose into the wind and nailed her down the airstrip. Unfortunately, we had started this at about mid strip and it was soon obvious that even if we did get her off the ground we would not clear the trees at the end of the runway. We aborted the take off and throttled back, full flaps and brakes on. Alberto slowed her down enough to pull a 180-degree turn. He nailed it again and we flew to the leeward end of the runway. We slowed her down and did another 180-degree turn. Now we had the whole runway with our nose into the wind.

The engines didn't sound right though, so Alberto hit the primers and the mixture controls while switching the magnetos to flush and backfire the engines. They cleared and sounded better so we nailed the engine to W.O.T. (wide open throttle) and started for another attempt to take off. Even the airspeed Pitot tube was plugged and we could only guess our speed. It didn't matter; the engines were completely loaded and misfiring severely by then, and though we were moving quickly, we could not feel her lift enough to even stretch her landing gear. We were screwed. Even with her modifications the "Dakota" just could not get enough air into the engines to produce the 1,200 HP needed per engine to lift us out of there. We aborted take off for the second and final time.

We got out of the plane and pulled our t-shirts over our heads to cover our hair. We put our bandanas over our nose and mouth. We told the locals to run for cover and to clean it off themselves, but they were too busy jumping around in it. This was something they had never seen before and like children they were amazed and playing in it. There was nothing we could do to reinstate discipline and common sense.

The next day many of the workers were sick and Alberto and I agreed that all was lost. We organized a donkey train and loaded up all of the pot from the airplane and some that was already baled and sealed up for transport. We had about 18,000 pounds out of a possible 120,000 pounds. We headed for the coast.

We were now back to the original methods that we had used when we started a few years before. We had to organize a donkey train and load all of the bales on donkeys and make our way to the coast. It took two days to arrange the 60+ donkeys needed to make the move. Now we had a 230-mile journey to start and we were hardly physically fit or supplied for the task at hand. Alberto was in for the experience of his life. I made contact with C.K. and Mike on the Polar Sea in Aruba from a radio in a friend's plane in El Banco. We were telling this incredible story that no one could perceive, nor wanted to believe. I admit that I couldn't believe it myself. It was like a bad dream.

We finally met up with the crew two weeks later in Riohacha and loaded the Polar Sea. The crew knew that my story was for real, as we loaded only a fraction of what we usually did. I showed Mike & C.K. my clothes and they told me to get rid of them as that orange powder was in fact Agent Orange, the same defoliant they used in Vietnam. It could cause cancer. I sat silently motionless as my eyes began to water up. All I could think about was all of those indigenous residents of the Medellín Valley who would suffer and die over the next few years. I had just witnessed and escaped a massive genocide. Why had we declared war on Colombia? Who authorized it? Why was there no news coverage about this atrocity? Where was the logic behind such a heinous act of human and ecological destruction? It would be 20 years before the truth would come out by disgruntled CIA operatives who became whistle blowers. We were out of business in one fell swoop.

When I came back to California I told Ray and Dan what happened. They said that they believed me, but I could see in their eyes that it was too fantastic for them to comprehend. They never questioned what happened to the load as Alberto was there to confirm my story. No one lost any money, since they only owed for what I had brought in. They had gotten so used to the easy money that it was difficult for many of the Detroit boys to accept that the ride was over. It was hard for me to accept it and I had been there!

I was pretty sick now from exhaustion, insomnia, and probably from the Agent Orange. I had lost a lot of weight, and when I got back to California I found out that Eileen had taken off with Dan's brother, sold our house and took one of my dogs along with the V35B Bonanza airplane I had bought her. Dan's brother had also taken my Kenworth truck to make the move, adding insult to injury.

The Miyako Hotel

I was wandering around carrying two Halliburton aluminum suitcases full of stacks of $100 bills. I was in a state of shock due to the events of the last few weeks. I was in a cocaine stupor, migrating from one hotel to another. As far as Ray and Don were concerned I was MIA (missing in action). They had flown in to San Francisco and rented some suites at the Japanese cultural center of the Miyako Hotel. The boys flew in from Detroit, Texas, and Louisiana for a party. Danny contacted the dispatchers at the major cab companies and offered all of the cab drivers in San Francisco $10,000 cash to the first one that could find me. Those must have been some skills he had learned as a teamster back in the Motor City.

I was walking by the herring boats at Fisherman's Wharf near Alioto's Restaurant when a cab pulled up and asked if I was Captain Duke. I asked why, and he said a man named Dan had given specific instructions to find me, to pick me up, and take me to the Miyako Hotel. I got in the cab and we headed off for the hotel. At the desk I was escorted to the suites. They had rented the whole 7th floor, and only registered guests could access this area. The security was intense. I entered the room and saw Dan and Ray by the window. They were glad to see me and were curious as to how I was holding up. I wanted to kick Dan's ass, and do even worse to his brother, but they were smart enough to not have him there. What had happened, *happened,* and no matter how mad I was, nothing was going to change it. I had no other choice but to bite the bullet and move on.

The next thing I knew people came in from both sides of the room from the adjoining suites. There were the boys from Texas, my crew, associates from Detroit and Ann Arbor and fellow Californians.

There were a lot of good friends in that room, but it was kind of like a wake. Even though everyone was having a good time, we were in fact celebrating the end of an era. Only Alberto and I fully realized the price that had been paid for their wealth and power. It could only be measured by the gallons of blood that had been spilt over the last five years, and the body count (yet to be tallied) of the hundreds of native Colombians that would soon die from the side effects of the orange herbicide they ingested. To this day I struggle with all of this.

As I sat in the back of the room on a couch by the wall people would come over, sit, talk some small talk and leave. Then these two beautiful girls sat down and asked who I was and why I was so quiet. It made me paranoid at first, as I was not a dashing figure like my colleagues. In fact every time a beautiful girl even talked to me I just assumed she must be an undercover F.B.I. or D.E.A. agent trying to get close to me for information, or even worse to take me into custody. After all I was still wanted in Michigan and probably many more places. Fred came over and sat with us, and went on to introduce us. He explained that I was the Captain who hauled all the pot that all of these people sold. I still didn't know what Fred was up to, or why he would say such a thing. Maybe he was trying to impress these two girls, or maybe he was just trying to pretend that he and I were long time best friends. I never figured it out. The more the party went on, the more out of place I felt, and the girls picked up on that quickly.

The blonde was Patricia and the Asian girl was Kim. They were good friends and lived in San Francisco. Patricia wore Charles Jordan shoes, Gloria Vanderbilt Blue Jeans that looked like they were painted on. She wore mink coats that were custom made from blue jean and Renaissance Fair patterns.

They spent all the time with me while I was there. This party went on for almost a week. When you got tired (or whatever) you would just go to your suite for a while to sleep, shower, or whatever, and just return at a later time. So I excused myself and went off to one of the suites. I still had those suitcases full of money to deal with, so I slid them under the bed.

I decided to take a shower, but when I went entered the bathroom I noticed that besides a shower there was also a Japanese bath, which was over 4 feet deep. This seemed like a more relaxing idea so I turned on the water and went back into the main room to roll a joint while it filled up.

To my surprise Ray was there with Patricia and Kim. He asked why I had left the party, and if I was all right. So I sat down at the table, and they joined me. I rolled up some Thai stick, and had Kim draw out some lines of Peruvian flake cocaine from a bag that I had in my coat pocket.

This was the real flake that looked like pure white glistening shale that reflected every color of the spectrum depending on how the light hit it. They had heard about it, but never seen it before.

I told Ray that here in the U.S. I am a fugitive. I had reconstructed a new life down in the Caribbean and now all that was destroyed. My risks and efforts had made everyone rich, and while they could return to their lives, I was still on the run. Ray told me that I needed to take some time off and get some rest and that we would talk later, and then he left.

It did not take much for Patricia and Kim to coax me into the Japanese tub. They were more than willing and capable to help me relax. After the bath, Kim gave me a massage and we all went to bed to get some rest – really! After all the party was still going on.

During the night I kept waking up and staring out the window into the city. I felt like an alien here, and for some reason I did not feel safe in America any more. For the first time in my life I felt ashamed to be an American, and was contemplating Canadian citizenship. The veil of innocence had been lifted from me during my exploits in the Medellín Valley. I was now fully aware that all wars, whether national, or political, and even the war on drugs were no more than an exercise in economics. Wars have nothing to do with humanitarian crusades the "powers that be" may try to convince you of as to their objective. The primary collateral damage is human life itself, the most of which is innocent families that are caught in the middle of the conflict.

As I smoked a joint I could feel someone behind me. It was Patricia, as Kim was still asleep. I guess she awoke when I got up and I was becoming a curiosity to her. She said that she could see that I was different from the rest of the group. I really think she was sincere to this day. So I opened up and we talked till we saw the sun come up. We went out for breakfast, and on the way back we stopped at some stores that she suggested and I bought some clothes. I had nothing except for those two suitcases full of money, not even a toothbrush. It was noon by the time we returned to the Miyako and the party was in full swing. Room service had just delivered a smorgasbord of shrimp, lobster, crab, *escargot*, salads, truffles and the like. There were cases of *Dom Pérignon*, and other French wines. Kim greeted us and asked where we had been, and then Patricia and her went off to talk. I looked for Ray.

I found him and we went onto the balcony for privacy. I told him that I was thinking of getting a bigger boat that was somewhere around 260 feet in length. The boat I had in mind was a yacht from the 1950's that had been built in Norway. She looked like a miniature cruise ship. It could have a helipad installed on the after deck, and my plan was to run Thai sticks from Asia. These would be long trips and this yacht could provide the accommodations and amenities that would support good crew morale.

I would be able to live on board and not worry about the constant danger of being a fugitive. She could be anchored in non-extradition harbors, and follow the summer seasons globally. There were more than enough cabins to provide accommodations for any visitors. Her cargo hold was more than adequate to contain a couple of automobiles and a couple of recreational watercraft. The helicopter would provide service to shore. I was prepared to separate myself from land and develop smuggling routes coordinated with strategies that would eliminate luck, but would rather be calculated risks. Ray could hear the urgency in my voice.

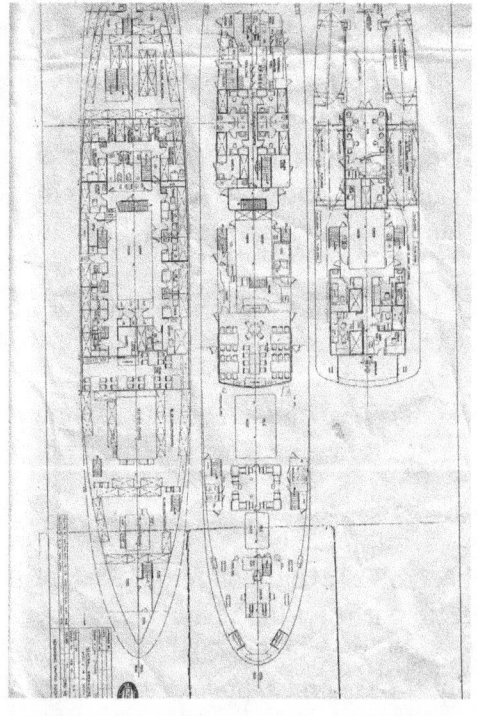

Plans for the boat under renovation

My definition of a smuggler was quite simple, "A person engaged in international trade of diversified commodities without recognition of geographical boundaries or human governments, who would supply the needs of people based upon the dedicated moral responsibility to preserve life and welfare." Ray liked my philosophy and encouraged me to proceed with my plans.

The Miyako Hotel

As I returned to the celebration I did not like what I saw, nor what I heard. My spirit was grieved as I watched my friends conduct being reduced to debauchery from the use of recreational drugs, alcohol, and their arrogance. They were treating some of the guests and the caterers and hotel personnel as if they were less than human. This included some public displays of sexual activity. I decided to return to my suite being followed by Patricia and Kim. They could tell that something was upsetting me and asked if I wanted to get away. I was curious as to what they had in mind.

The girls suggested we go to Lake Tahoe, as they knew of a chalet that was one of many owned by the Gessler Jewelry family. This was a time-share that I could rent for a couple of weeks. I was pretty excited about this and agreed. We made arrangements for the Hansa to fly us there and I told Ray I would meet him at his house in Belvedere in a couple of weeks.

Lake Tahoe was beautiful, and I could finally relax. The Swiss chalet had 3 floors with a natural rock cliff waterfall that was over 30 feet tall that emptied in to a hot tub at the base. I spent about 10 days there with them, and started to gain a perspective on my future. I called a friend of mine in Healdsburg who was a realtor, and told him to find me a suitable house. He knew of an "A" frame built on rock in an isolated area of Sonoma County that he could not sell, because of its remote location, and difficult access to it. It was located on Tarwater Road between Santa Rosa and St. Helena. The place was perfect.

I purchased the property as soon as I saw it and bought a new 4-wheel drive Ford Econoline van, as the road I lived on was no more than a rocky fire trail. There was a creek that bordered one side of the property that was more like a cliff, and the rest of the property was old growth redwood trees that were huge. I can only imagine that the only reason that they had not been logged out years ago was that there would not have been any path to harvest them out. Patricia and Kim had returned to San Francisco after we exchanged numbers.

After I moved in and settled the house, I got the crew together to take the Polar Sea back through the Panama Canal, and to the West Coast again. I formed a towing company called Maritime Services International, and we went into legitimate towing. We would work the West Coast of California all the way to Dutch Harbor, Alaska, doing tows that nobody really wanted. It wasn't like we intended to get rich, as most of us were all set. We just liked the old boat and she had served us well over the years. I took a sabbatical from the smuggling trade for a while, and was primarily involved with the renovations being done on the new boat in Seattle. She needed a lot of work, as her glory days had long gone by. I had only paid around $300,000 for her and could justify a little over $1 million for her restoration and modifications. Ray had taken an interest in the project, and had provided a seven-digit donation to ensure its success. Restored and seaworthy she would be worth several million dollars, as she had a Lloyds 100 A1 rating. The Norwegians really knew how to build quality boats that would last a lifetime, and the lines of her shape were timeless. She resembled the Christine Onassis in size and shape. She would fit right in with the rest of the yachts anchored off the coast of Greece in the Mediterranean.

I formed the corporate office in Portland, Oregon listing my homeport in Seattle at the Lake Union Drydock. I leased office spaces and Pier 3 in San Francisco, at the Embarcadero.

Patty was now coming to the house for two or three days at a time. We had become close and she became my confidante. She was extremely smart and had the skills of perceiving people. I seemed to be more peaceful when she was around. When I would go to Seattle to inspect the work being completed on the new boat she would travel with me. Ray would often meet us there, and we would conduct our review of the progress and quality of the craftsmanship being completed by the shipyard, while Patricia and Ray's girlfriend would go shopping. This was the pattern of our lives for about six months.

Then one day I got a call from Patricia saying that she urgently needed to talk to me. I told her to meet me at the Tarwater Road property. When she arrived I could see that she was upset. We went inside and sat down in the living room overlooking the pool and creek. While I was starting a fire in the this huge fireplace she told me that Kim and her had an argument and that she wanted to talk to me before anyone else did. At this point I was curiously confused.

After a glass of red wine she began to explain that she really had sincere feelings for me. She continued by revealing that when Kim, her, and I met at the Miyako that it was not by coincidence. Kim and her were in fact call girls. They had met Fred and Danny months ago through an elite escort service. The boys were concerned about my disappearance and mental state, and came up with the idea of hiring two escorts to keep an eye on me. Our chance meeting was in fact an orchestrated business arrangement and the girls were each making over $3,000 per week as a retainer for whatever services were provided. Patricia said that after the third month she refused to accept any more money as she felt that her and I had something going on. Well, Kim was either jealous or upset about the termination of this lucrative arrangement, and when she found out that Patricia and I were still seeing each other she threatened to tell me everything. Patricia had talked about this situation with Ray before coming to see me. Ray advised her that it was best to tell me the truth before someone else did. She also said that if I had any doubts as to the accuracy of what she telling me, that I was to call Ray.

I was in a complete state of shock! I said to her, "I knew the first day we met that something was up, but I flowed with it and ended up letting my guard down." Now I was confused as to whether Patricia loved me, my money, or my status within these power brokers. I called Ray and he confirmed that everything she said was true. As for me it was already too late. I had these real feelings for Patricia and love never keeps count of the injury…it bears all things, hopes all things, endures all things. Though things were never ever the same between Dan and Fred and me, I know they may have meant well, but somewhere they crossed a line of trust that could not be rescinded.

Patricia and I set up housekeeping at the Chalet and she introduced me to her daughter Erica, the child from a previous relationship. Erica was 3 years old at the time. For the first time in a long time I now felt complete, and I started to separate myself from the organization. Only Ray and I stayed close as I even distanced myself from Pete and Kate. Money had tainted the relationship of our original group and now I felt more like a commodity than a friend to those people. They were all financially comfortable due to the risks that my crew and I had taken over the last few years – not to mention all those who perished in Colombia. The collateral damage was monumental and I was having an epiphany. The reciprocity had reached its consummation.

Soon we leased a villa in Woodside, California, near Palo Alto so that Erica could start pre-school and develop neighborhood friends. The property was the estate of Pierre De Satel who had been the Chairman of the Board for TWA until his passing on. I took a lease on the place until the estate could be settled by his heirs. That would take a few years. In the meantime Patricia and I set up a new image for me as the C.E.O. of a respectable company engaged in overseas towing contracts. It was a good cover and we had the self discipline to pull it off. I now wore bankers gray with a pin-stripe instead of blue jeans and T-shirts. Patricia traded in her wardrobe for basic black and a string of pearls. I was actually attending PTA meetings at the Montessori school where we had enrolled Erica. She was a year ahead of the other children as I did not know how to raise a child. I just treated and talked to Erica like an adult and we got along very well. Being surrounded by our friends she did not behave like the average child. She was more aware of life than some of my acquaintances.

At Thanksgiving when Patricia's parents came out to our place for dinner, she took her mother's and father's coats to hang them up in the cloakroom by the front door. When Patricia opened the door to the room a box fell out and on down to the floor with stacks of $100 bills spilling everywhere. Erica ran up, grabbed the box and started stacking the money back in to it saying, "Don't worry, Grampy, this happens all the time." It was very quiet during dinner as Patricia's father was the head of commercial loans at Wells Fargo in downtown San Francisco. This type of banking practice was unheard of in his circle. He never commented about this incident – ever – but you could tell by the look on his face that a lot was going on inside his head.

Later that week, Mila, Patricia's mother, called and asked me to come by her house alone. When I arrived she was ready to go and suggested we go have lunch. At the Cliff House we were making small talk when out of the blue she said, "Duke, if you need to keep something safe or available in an emergency then you should give it to me to put away. Do not mention to Fred we had this conversation." I was stunned, but it made solid sense and I took her up on the offer. The next day I dropped off a couple of boxes and a briefcase full of diplomatic passports.

Dan's Overdose

The next couple of months went well for us until one day I got a phone call from Ray. He told me that Dan and his wife had been found in a hotel room dead from a heroin overdose. Ray wanted me to fly in to Aspen, Colorado and identify the bodies for the coroner. The Hansa was ready to take me, meanwhile our attorneys had made arrangements to forward some cash to the coroner to help clear this up. All they needed was someone to sign papers to confirm identities. I was more than apprehensive, as both Ray and I knew that Dan didn't use heroin. None of us did. We were potheads who would occasionally binge a few days on some good coke. I flew in to Aspen, and was picked up by Dan's limo driver.

He took me to the coroner's office and after I showed them some identification, and established my relationship to the deceased, I was taken into a room with two cadavers. The coroner folded back the sheet that was covering one of the bodies, and sure enough it was Dan. I confirmed his identity. Next he flipped back the sheet covering the second corpse and I took a good look, but something was wrong. I pulled the sheet down farther and sure enough there was a tattoo of Speedy Gonzales stoned and smoking a joint. This was NOT Dan's wife. It was her twin sister! I informed the coroner of this and began to ask him questions. In their personal effects was over $8,000 in cash. This was not a robbery, but foul play had left its stench all over this situation. I had the limo driver take me out to Dan's place, and sure enough his wife's personal items had been hastily packed - and so were items of clothing that were removed from the dresser of Dan's four year old son. Evidently, they were alive and hiding from something, somewhere. I flew back to California to meet with Ray, as I did not feel safe to use the phones. Dan's sister-in-law was just the opposite of Dan's wife. She was wild and dated biker types and whatever. Dan was always getting her out of some kind of trouble, and it seemed to be on a weekly basis. As he put it, he did not just marry his wife, he married her whole family. She lived off of handouts of cash from Dan. It would be easy to mistake the two girls, as I used to have to second-guess all the time.

I told Ray what was up and we both came to the same conclusion. Dan must have been meeting her to give her some money. There were a lot of questions to still be answered. What was the deal with the heroin? Why was the cash still there? What motive was there? Where were Dan's wife and son?

It was then that Ray told me that Dan had been having some problems with the F.B.I., and the C.I.A. Counter Measures Security Systems Company had been detecting and unhooking bugs placed by those agencies in embassies, at the U.N. and in Washington, D.C. Ray and Pete told me that Dan's company had even made the cover of Time magazine, when they found a Russian bug in the Great Seal of the United States in our embassy in Germany.

Counter Measures was started by Dave (my counter intelligence person) at the University of Ann Arbor when I was isolating the THC molecule years before. Dave had been a student who was enrolled in the mathematics department, and he was also taking electronic sciences and manufacturing sciences. I got my first radar detector from him. He also set up all our radios, and was my ace in the hole, as he slept in a room that had a radio monitoring a certain frequency 24 hours a day. He started a small company called Counter Measures Security Systems to combat industrial espionage. This company grew quickly when Dave and Dan met, as Dan supplied all the necessary funds for prototype building, testing, and development. They were eavesdropping on big brother, and big brother did not like it one bit. Agents had approached Dan to sell the company, or work for them. Dan just laughed and told them that there was an unlimited worldwide market for counter measure systems, and it would be stupid to turn it over to just one group. While each side was bugging the other side, Dan and Dave would be paid to locate and unhook the devices, and would be collecting from all of them. This was the first that I had heard of this, and it made the hair stand up on the back of my neck. I wondered what other secrets Ray was "protecting" me from.

About a month later Ray called and asked me to meet him in New Orleans. I arranged for the Hansa and flew in at night. We met in the old French Quarter at the Le Booze bar. Ray was telling me about his new toy. It was a 50-foot Viking sport-fisherman with twin engines and it could cruise in excess of 45 knots. She had a pair of turbo-charged

Dan's Overdose

Caterpillar diesels. He wanted me to deliver the boat to the Bahamas. I told him that I would have to refuel in Marathon Key, Florida as that was almost the limit of the safe range for that boat. I told him that I could make the 1,100 mile trip to Rum Cay in a little over 24 hours. We went down to the marina and I put some supplies on board, checked the boat out thoroughly, extra oil, charts, and cash for the fuel dock in Marathon. I asked Ray what was in all the dive bags that were stuffed in the lockers. He showed me. It was money. Billy would go with me. He was one of our truck drivers and a very close friend to Ray. I had known him as long as I had known Ray. He was a year younger than me and usually stayed in the shadows. His Peterbilt always transported Ray's portion of our loads. We cast-off and left in the Viking, while Ray went to the airport to head for the Bahamas in the Hansa.

I told Billy that I was nervous taking a brand new – unproven boat out for such a long distance run. Even though she was of the finest quality and construction, and had impeccably reliable diesels, this was no more than a break in cruise for her. Emphasis on break. We needed to be alert on the gauges, and take alternate visits to the engine room to check for any trouble by smell or visual inspection. We would do an oil and filter change in Marathon Key. I did not bring up the subject of Dan, as I was not aware of whether Billy knew about it. The subject was very heavy on my mind.

We cruised into Marathon about 10am and pulled up to the fuel dock. I arranged for an oil change and we topped off the fuel tanks. Our cover story to the compliments made by the fuel-jockeys about this brand new boat, was that we were delivering it to a charter company in the Bahamas. We then went into the cafe to get some much needed breakfast.

A little after our breakfast we were ready to start the next leg of our trip. A complete inspection of the boat during this service revealed that she was a sound vessel even if her exhaust manifolds were no longer pure white. The smell of new paint was gone from the engine room and I was feeling more comfortable now that she was a seasoned vessel.

Our 13:00 hour departure meant that we would be shooting through the Andros Island Channel and into the "tongue of the ocean" at around 17:00 hours, or sunset. That would be perfect timing for us, as the sun would be at our backs, and visibility will be greatly enhanced. There are a lot of small local fishing boats in this channel of wood construction and they do not show up very well on radar. The last thing we needed was an incident with the locals with a load of money to explain if we were boarded. After Andros passage we would swing southeast and pick up Great Guana Cay in about 3 hours - and then the final leg to Rum Cay. With any luck we should be there at about 23:00 hours, or 11pm.

We tied up at Port Nelson in Rum Cay at about midnight. We had lost some time running against the tide flow of the channel. Ray was very happy to see us, and we all sat down for some conch chowder and lobster. Billy and I were beat, and soon returned to the boat to get some sleep.

We awoke the next day to a pounding on the cabin as Ray was already up. He had made arrangements for Billy to return to New Orleans and I was to stay for a couple of days to do some – uh- fishin', yeah, that's it – fishin'. We saw Billy off at the airstrip then Ray and I got ready to go fishin'.

We went to his place on the West side of the island. It was a new place, ocean front property in a private part of the island. There was a long dock that went out into the channel. So after lunch we brought the Viking around and tied her up to her new home. The scene was picture post-card perfect – other than the fishing gear that Ray handed me - TWO SHOVELS! At dark we were going to bury those dive-bags. I evidently was the only one Ray trusted to do this and to this day I have yet to figure out why. Maybe Billy was too close to Ray for him to feel comfortable with that kind of information. This was Ray's choice and I felt that it would be inappropriate to question his reasons. It didn't take long, and then it was time to relax. We sat out on the porch with his newborn daughter and talked till we saw the glow of the sun rising. Ironically it was red. (Red at night sailors delight, red in the morning sailor take warning). Was this an omen? Two months from that moment in time I would be pondering that question again.

I flew back to California the next day in the Hansa stopping twice for fuel. I was tired but it was great to see Erica and Patricia again. I told them that Ray had a new place and we would take an annual trip to the Bahamas to visit them and not have to stay in a hotel. Erica thought that was great, but Patricia was concerned about some calls from Fred, Pete, Jim and others who wanted to arrange a meeting in San Francisco. I called Pete back and told him to set it up and call me back as to where and when. I would be there.

About a week later we all met at the Fairmont Hotel in San Francisco, but we moved the meeting across the way to the Californian Hotel Suite for security. The whole crew was there and not to my surprise Ray wasn't, neither was Billy. Our last talk on the porch at Rum Cay was about knowing when to get out while you were ahead. There was a lot of rumor and talk about Dan's death and I was able to separate the fact from the fiction, due to the fact that I was the only who had been there. The bottom line of this meeting was that the boys wanted to make one last run.

First of all, there is a superstition among smugglers that is centuries old. Never ever set sail on "one last run" as it probably – inevitably will be your last run. You will either sink, get caught, or worse get killed. It is some kind of undocumented jinx, for no one ever sees or hears from the boat or crew, and they are eventually forgotten. If you retire - do it after you finish your last trip!

Second, I wasn't going to work without Ray, nor would I consider a trip without David monitoring intelligence. He was nowhere to be found, and to this day I do not know of what may have happened to him, nor does anyone else have any info. Dave just vanished!

Third, the product in Colombia was now tainted with Agent Orange. The pot that was coming out of there recently, by our competitors, was giving people a sore throat and congested lungs, and it tasted terrible. The only other Colombian reefer was the coastal reefer off the western pacific slopes and it is really bad. I was not going to do a West Coast Colombian trip. The chances of being detected were too staggering to even consider.

This did not sit well with them, and to my disbelief, one by one, each of them attempted to go around the other's backs to try to negotiate a private deal with me as a 50/50 partner. Finally Pete sat down with me and started this conversation of how we have worked together for all these years, going all the way back to the Katie L. and the draft evaders. This was really stickin' it to me - to entwine sentimentalities with a business proposition. I told him that none of this was rational, and while they would be sitting here in the states, my crew and I would be crawling into the belly of the beast. So, in no uncertain terms I said, "No way," and that this conversation is over. Before I could get up to leave Pete threw a glass of wine in my face.

I was really upset now. What had happened to this group? Not that long ago we all got together to risk our lives and freedom, not for the money, but because the high that we got from all of this was beyond what they were trying to get from their cocaine and wine. Their souls were empty, and they could not fill them with all the money they had. The rush for life that they had become addicted to, was now feeding off of me like a school of piranhas. Ray was right, and I stormed out. I jumped in to my '30 Ford Coupe and burned rubber till the next block.

I got back to Woodside, California and told Patricia what had happened. She said that she saw it coming a long time ago – when we met. She couldn't tell me then because it was not her place, but she knew I would figure it out in due time. She recommended that I should count my blessings, focus on my business, and that, oh by the way, she was pregnant, very pregnant.

Ray's Death

About a month went by, and one night around 4am, California time, I got a phone call from Ray's wife. She was hysterical. She had returned to the Rum Cay house with the baby after visiting with her mother in N.Y.C. only to find Ray lying on the floor in the den, dead from a heroin overdose. She would have called me sooner but she was under house arrest and being questioned by the authorities. The Bahamas are under Parliamentary Law and this was a pretty serious matter to them. This was completely absurd because Ray never used heroin! For Ray to use heroin would be to violate all that Ray and his wife preached and lived. Neither of them would consume anything that was toxic or was not healthful.

My mind was reeling. I did not know what to think. I asked her if anything was disturbed on the property. She said no. She said that she was going to do what Ray had told her to do, should something out of the ordinary occur, and this was what he had meant. Ray always had back-up plans. We were both Virgos and we thought a lot alike. She was packing the baby's things and would head for their manor in France.

I didn't know what to think. Ray and I buried over $50 million (I choose not to state the full amount) in cash, and only he and I know about it, and where it was buried. Ray never told his wife so that she could not be used as a pawn in the event of a hostile situation. The money was not dug up, or she would have mentioned this large hole in the garden. So again, this was not about the money. First Dan overdoses, then Ray was found dead from a heroin overdose, and neither of them ever used heroin. There was no motive for any of our associates as the money was still buried there. It was more than obvious that these were murders - made to look like reckless recreational drug use that ended in death.

It was time for damage control. I started looking for another house. We had been there too long and I no longer felt we were safe there. Patricia found us a brand new constructed multi-story unit on the top of Diamond Heights in San Francisco. We moved there immediately. I had Bekins movers remove and store all of our furniture in a warehouse that was from the Woodside property. We bought all new furnishings and appliances, assumed new identities and eliminated a paper trail.

It was the beginning of December, and Patricia, Erica, and I had settled in to our new home. On a clear day I could see almost all the way down to Pier 3 where my offices were. My old crew was long gone other than my chief engineer. Mike lived in Mill Valley and he had sentimental feelings for this old tugboat. Her Superior VDMSS diesel was his baby, and after thousands of miles, and hours attending to her every need he just could not conceive a union, paid-by-the-hour, engineer replacing him and taking care of this antique piece of history that was around forty years old. Mike and I shared a common respect for "old school" technologies, and mechanics that were superb in design, and construction, providing reliable continuous service over decades with minimum maintenance or overhead. We loved this old boat. The rest of the crew, including C.K., my first mate, had all gone on to better things.

Engine room of the POLAR SEA

The 23rd of December 1979 Patricia went into labor and 15 hours later Tara Denise was born. Wow! I was officially a father and this changed everything. To look at her with her tiny hands and feet, and her deep stare directly into my eyes was an experience that I had never felt before. The timing may not have been the best with all of this chaos around me, and my status as a fugitive, but when is it ever ideal to have children? You just have to roll with it and you re-adjust your life accordingly as you would with any other situation. Tara turned out to be daddy's little girl, and we spent a lot of time together. On days when Erica was not in school, I would take her down to the tug with me. She had the run of the boat, and the new crew was wrapped around her finger.

Otto (l) and Erica on board the POLAR SEA

My able bodied seaman (ABS) was Otto. During World War II he had been a Navy Blue Jacket. His duty on the Polar Sea was the chief boatswain mate, responsible for the other ABS's, the hull, deck, and equipment. He taught Erica everything from tying knots to winch maintenance. They were an inseparable pair, and I knew she was safe when on the boat. Mariner crews are much like a family. We share food, we work while others rest, we serve watches, and we operate as a team, but most of all we share the responsibility of the boat, as without her we are nothing.

I had just become acclimated to the arrival of Tara when Patricia informed me that she was pregnant again. I was in shock. Life was coming at me fast and deep. I was no longer an independent purveyor of diversified commodities. I now had responsibilities that exceeded my personal plan and endeavors. I still had a 260 foot yacht being renovated in Seattle, and she was at least a year away from sea trials. I hadn't even picked out a name for her yet. I felt much like the blues guitarist Robert

Johnson must have felt just before he sold his soul to the devil at the crossroads. "Life is what happens to you while you're busy making other plans." - John Lennon.

That spring Patricia received a call from her mom and she turned ghostly pale and dropped the phone. Evidently that afternoon some men in suits and sunglasses with federal identification entered Fred's office at the main Wells Fargo branch in San Francisco to show him a picture. It was the picture of a slender man wearing cut-off shorts, a bandana on his head and a pair of Ray-Ban 5024 sunglasses. He was wearing two shoulder holsters with 45 automatics and in his right hand was a Thompson machine gun. He was standing on a pile of burlap bales in a dug out canoe. Fred said that the man did not look familiar. The agents informed him that they had information that the man was living with his daughter. They left him their card and told him to contact them if the man in the picture turned up.

We abandoned the house in Diamond Heights and headed for Stockton. We stayed at a hotel that night, and the next day we went to a realtor and rented another house in a development on a cul-de-sac. Just like before we had a moving company pack up and store all of our household belongings. I had a friend of mine, Captain Al, who ran a tug in S.F. Bay, take the Polar Sea to Seattle. I needed to buy some time to gather good intelligence in order to make some serious decisions. What was going on? At least no one knew where we were now. I needed some reliable information - and quick.

I headed up to Napa, California to see Pete and Kate. I went out to their farm and we made attempts to set our differences from the past aside. This was a situation that involved all of us. Who took that picture, and when? It was obvious that it was when we were hauling those large loads off Cabo de la Aguja in the mid 70's. Pete and Kate said that they could not help as they were separate from the old crowd.

My Arrest

I returned to Stockton and we established a new profile and identity there. Things were quiet, and I was able to spend time with Erica and Tara. Tara was up and active while Patricia was getting bigger. Gypsy, our Doberman pinscher was Tara's favorite toy. The two were always together. Gypsy never left her side. It was as if she felt Tara belonged to her. When company would come by she would always get between strangers and Tara. It was not uncommon to find Tara asleep on the floor with a bottle in her mouth, and either Gypsy wrapped around her or Tara using Gypsy for a pillow. When we would pick Tara up to put her in her crib, Gypsy would give us a dirty look and follow us into Tara's room. I felt secure again with the feeling of a fresh start.

In May, 1981, Ryan was born. I was so excited as I now had a son. I had deep regrets as to the fact that my children could not have my last name. It is the curse that is inherited when your dad is a fugitive on the run. I was always hoping to be able to hire an attorney to fix this mess, but who could I trust? I spent a lot of nights just sitting in the dark and thinking about it. I never showed that side to my children or to Patricia. I always appeared to have it all under control – but that was the furthest from the truth. The shit was about to hit the fan.

One morning Patricia got a phone call from her mother, and we were informed that the feds had come by their house to talk to Fred and her. They asked if we had been in contact with them, and they said no. The feds said that they thought I may be in the Sacramento area. Stockton is only 45 miles from Sacramento and that was too close. To our advantage, Mila had called us from a payphone at the San Francisco Zoo where she worked. Patty and I made arrangements and a game plan for our Nanny, Cheryl, to watch the house and to take care of Erica and Tara. We grabbed Ryan, put him in the 1930 coupe, and headed for Mexico.

After getting to Ensenada we checked in to a hotel and got some much needed sleep. The next morning I leased an estate about 10 miles southwest of Ensenada. There wasn't even a town there, but the beautiful villa had a gated road and courtyard all around it. On the coast, secluded, I could see for a long way off for any incoming traffic. It is amazing that you don't need references or credit checks when you give a year's rent in advance. All we had to do was return to California, pack up the kids, call the moving and storage company, and bail out. I would operate the Polar Sea out of Ensenada, and when the other boat was ready I would have her delivered down there. We could move on board and load up with our small boats and cars and take off. That was not going to be the case though.

Robert in front of Hussong's in Ensenada, Baja California, Mexico

We returned to Stockton a few days later and I noticed a Cadillac parked near the cul-de-sac that was in visual range of our house. I took a good look at the driver as we drove by, and he was trying to look the other way. It looked real suspicious, and the driver looked pretty sleazy. I immediately thought of Dan and Ray.

When I pulled into the garage and went into the house I asked Cheryl if she had noticed the Cadillac. She said that it had been there for 2 days now. I immediately started a fire in the fireplace - burning charts, papers, pictures – man I was burning everything. Patricia was packing the children's things so she could drop them at her mom's. The plan was that I would make a break for Mexico in the coupe after I delivered them to Patricia's mother's house - and we would meet up later. I parked our Cadillac in the garage and started loading the suitcases with the bare essentials she would need for the exodus. Mike came by and picked up the coupe and drove it back to Marin.

The next morning Patricia, Erica, Tara, Ryan, and I got in the Cadillac and we headed for Interstate 5 south. We were being followed by that other Caddy but now there were a few more vehicles with him. It was obvious that we were being tailed, and therefore in some serious trouble, so I accelerated to over 100 miles an hour. As I came up over a rise I was relieved to see the CHP on the side of the road. I slowed down and then I realized that there were 6 CHP vehicles on one side of the road and 5 on the other. They all came onto the freeway and boxed me in a V formation. Then I heard the helicopters. Interstate 5 was closed!

I came to a stop and we were surrounded by law enforcement officers with a lot of guns. Patricia looked at me, and I looked at her, and she asked if I was going to make a run for it. I said no. She was relieved. They told me to put my hands where they could see them and put my weapons on the dash. I complied by emptying my coat of ninja stars, push knives, tantos, etc. There was not enough room on the dashboard of the car for all of them. Erica was pulling more weapons out from under the seats and handing them to me. I don't know where she was coming up with them. She was reaching into the back seat, inside the armrest, everywhere. Evidently she had been stashing them over the last couple of months when her and I would take trips, and/or run errands. The cops were freaking out. Soon they dragged me out of the car to handcuff me and then took me to the county jail for booking. There would be no bond, and I would remain in custody until 1983.

I was transported by U.S. Marshals to Monroe County, Michigan on a United Airlines flight. That was before Con-Air. I was in Monroe, Michigan to be arraigned on the charges from D.T.'s nightmare, and then I was taken to Milan Federal Penitentiary for holding. Two days later I was taken to the Federal Building in Detroit, Michigan and arraigned on the smuggling charges. That is when I met Paul Borman who would be my attorney. He told me what was going on. I finally discovered what all had happened.

Cannabis Cowboy

It seems that after Pete threw the wine in my face at the California Hotel and I walked out, Fred and him decided to reform "the band." Pete went back to my hometown at Put-in-Bay and found my cousin Bill. Bill was operating the tug I used to run, and as the season was shutting down for the winter, would go out west to meet Fred and the rest of the crew. Bill met Fred, C.K. (my first mate) and a couple of the deck hands. They bought a fishing boat and went to Cabo Corrientes to pick up a load of low-grade coastal Colombian reefer. This was near the traffic area of the Panama Canal entrance at Panama. That area is heavily monitored by radar and patrol boats. Anyway, they got the load and headed north following the coast for a 3,500 mile run. You see, while Bill could operate a boat, he lacked the ability and training that I had acquired over the years of piloting most of Lake Erie. Pete just assumed that all of the island boys inherited these skills at birth. Not having deep-water navigation skills they had decided to use the long-range radar and the radio-direction-finder (RDF) to coastal navigate the entire route. They were not far enough out at sea and were under surveillance from the start. The next mistake was to unload in Long Beach. The feds followed their trucks to San Francisco, California, Houston Texas, N.Y.C., Detroit Michigan, and Seattle Washington. Then they followed their pickup truck campers to their destinations and then they sprang the trap.

Over a hundred people were indicted. That is not all of it. The guy who took the picture of me was James Keogh. He was one of Dan's boys, who owed Dan a lot of money - so I broke down and let him go with us on a trip in 1976, to earn some money as a bale handler, or a grunt. Evidently this was the most exciting experience of his life, so he concealed a Kodak 110 in his gear. My crew and I had this fear of cameras, or any other means of documenting our activities that could incriminate us at a later date in time. After the trip (maybe a year later), while he was partying with these hookers and some cocaine in a Detroit hotel, he got busted. They found pictures of me, the Aquarian Sea and who knows what else. That is what spearheaded the investigation. What is of interest here is that the feds figured out quickly that this current operation was not the crew who had been running all the reefer from the Caribbean and into the U.S. This group was a bunch of idiots who were not capable of developing or operating the sophisticated enterprise that they were looking for.

My Arrest

Under the new RICO (Racketeering Influenced Criminal Organization) statutes of 1980, they were all facing 20 to life! Yes, Pete, Fred, Bill, C.K., and James – and the rest of the 100 were in some deep-deep trouble. I never figured out all of who gave me up, but one of the many had to be Pete, as he was the last person I saw when I moved to Stockton, and none of the rest of them knew of my whereabouts. This fiasco had already gone down at the time that I had visited them in Napa. They were all under investigation, while many were in custody, and neither he nor Kate ever said a damn thing!

I was accused of running 27 trips out of Colombia between 1973 and 1978 at around 100,000 pounds per trip. There were no records, no evidence, and all they had was a picture of someone who might be me, standing on bales of something, in a dug-out canoe on the water.... somewhere.

Nevertheless I was arraigned on these charges. At my bond hearing the prosecutor complained that, "Mr. Schmidt is a Maritime Captain extraordinaire, and his abilities would allow him to flee our jurisdiction given anything that will float. He has contacts in many countries that do not share extradition treaties with the U.S. He is a smuggler, his great uncles were whiskey smugglers, and we have no doubt that his grandchildren will be interstellar plutonium smugglers!" The courtroom exploded in hysterical laughter and the judge reprimanded the prosecutor. Nonetheless, I did not receive a bond and I was returned to Milan.

The Deal

Two weeks went by and I was taken to the federal building again. I was escorted in chains to an office and Paul Borman, my attorney, was there with some brass from the Department of Defense. As I looked at them, all I could think of was how much more trouble I might be in. Borman explained to me that one of these officers was from the Coast Guard and the other one was from naval intelligence. It turns out that they were concerned with my ability to travel in and out of U.S. ports without clearing customs or being detected – not just once – but at my own discretion.

I immediately recognized the opportunity to make a bargain for my situation. I had intelligence that they wanted. So I decided to throw them a bone. I confidently asked them "Did you ever find the Joe Louis?" They did not know what I was talking about. So I told them to check their "hot sheets" from back in 1975. At that point I clammed up – meeting was over – and I was returned to Milan.

Less than a week later I was again taken to the federal building in Detroit – same room, same officers and the District Attorney and, of course, my attorney. The brass immediately asked what I knew about the Joe Louis. So I told them that when I found out that she was "hot" for gun running I disposed of her at the Monkey Island Coast Guard Station in Cameron, Louisiana. This made them upset due to my laughter, because I thought it was funny. They called me a liar, as there are no records of the Joe Louis, not even a registration since 1975. They had actually given her up for lost. I told them to physically check the docks down there and ask the personnel who take care of the boats to see if they remembered her. Interview was over.

Two days later they brought me back and wanted to know how I got the Joe Louis into the impound area without detection. I told them the whole story. They just shook their heads and walked into another room to talk. It seems that my antics had given the Navy officer an avenue to ridicule the Coast Guard officer. They returned to the room I was in, and I immediately asked them if the Coast Guard Cutter Dauntless was still breaking starboard propeller shafts at high speeds. Now they were looking at me very seriously. They asked what I had to do with the Dauntless. I said, "Not until you answer my question." The interview was over, and it was a Friday. I was returned to Milan and waited for Monday. I already knew they would be taking me to Detroit. That was a no brainer.

Well, I was wrong. They didn't come and get me until Wednesday. In that same room in Detroit they asked why or how I knew about the Dauntless' propulsion failures. I told them about Dauntless chasing me off the coast of Miami in the Straits of Florida between South Bimini and Turtle Rocks. This is what I told them:

We had seen her on radar and watched her change course in our direction. Don't know why, but it was obvious that she was following us because we had gradually arced our course off a few degrees at a time to the south. She was flanking our moves. I headed for the shoals and transferred all our fuel to the rear tanks to keep our propeller buried and raise the bow. We now drew 10 feet of water at the "shoe" under the propeller that hooks to the base of the rudder. We drew about 7 feet at the bow. If we hit bottom we would slide up without ripping her hull open. Then we would be able to abandon in our skiffs, which were very fast, and disappear into the many islands and lagoons.

The Dauntless was much faster than us, and she had alerted "Whiskey Oscar Mike" that she was in hot pursuit of a suspected smuggler. We started to plot her on radar and I turned up the sensitivity on the fathometer while diligently watching the graph. I called down to the engine room and told Mike what was going on and I needed more speed. He said he would raise the pyrometric temperature on the cylinders and switch over to used bunker oil. This was 40-weight ashless oil that we used to lubricate the main engine. It would give us some added horsepower and our exhaust would be black like a smoke screen. The sun was going down and we still had a twelve-mile lead.

Soon we were in the worst of the shoals, and Mike called up from the engine room to tell me that we were so close to the bottom that he could hear resonance from the coral reef under our hull and he could also hear shells being sucked through our propeller. I assured him that I was aware of the situation and I was carefully monitoring our course. He mumbled something about the lobster and crab needing hard hats.

106

The Deal

It wasn't long before we heard the whistle of an artillery shell over the pilothouse. It splashed and exploded about 100 yards in front of us. We looked back and could see the Dauntless fire another round. That one fell short. The next one would hit, as they now had our range.

I pulled the alarm for general quarters, and called down to the engine room to tell Mike to get his crew up on deck to prepare to abandon ship. The next shell would probably take out the pilothouse. I asked C.K. for a fix off the radar and alerted the crew to get the skiffs ready to launch. These were two Boston whalers: one 19 feet and one 15 feet with big Mercury outboards. We also had two Zodiak inflateables. The whalers could exceed speeds of 50kts in any sea, with an endurance of several hours. They were our last resort.

Then I heard the whistle of an incoming shell. I ran out of the pilothouse just in time to see it splash in our wake - close enough that we got wet from the explosion. The crew yelled, "They missed," but I said, "No, they never miss." I ran back in the pilothouse to the radar. I showed C.K. their position and he said that they must have stopped chasing us. I told him that they hadn't stopped – they ran aground. It was dusk and we disappeared just like the sun over the horizon.

The Dauntless hit the reef in full pursuit at mid-tide. She wasn't going anywhere for a while. She slid up on the shoals so far that she was stuck there for 3 days until the high tide on the rise of the full moon. She had buckled her hull under the starboard engine. They never reported the incident to "Whiskey Oscar Mike" in Miami to save their embarrassment. That is the time when she started snapping propeller shafts, as her starboard engine was no longer in line with her stuffing boxes. I am sure the engineers knew this, as the new vibration would be very annoying in the engine room. Their cups of coffee could not only stir themselves, but would also dance.

That was all the convincing that the interviewing brass needed. I asked for an attorney conference with Borman. The feds had seized all of my assets in vehicles, boats, bank accounts, etc. The only thing they didn't have was the 1930 coupe. That was safe with Mike in Marin.

I told Borman that I would tell them how I monitored them, my strategies, and times and dates. I would NOT divulge my crew nor implicate anyone else. This would be strictly a national security issue, not a witch-hunt. In return I wanted time served after they were satisfied, then I would walk. Here is what I told Borman:

I had a bank of scanners and each scanner was assigned to a major Coast Guard cutter. Every day the senior officer of the cutter would check in with her homeport early in the morning. They would relay their course, fuel supply, engineering reports, machinery parts needed, crew health, crew rotation, food stores, personal family information, and the like. If I monitored the radio activity of selected cutters in my area, I would know every detail of the condition of the cutter, personal details about her crew, her projected patrol strategies, and most of all when they would be heading in to port. When they were heading in you could time your entry to follow right behind them as they usually did not monitor any activity that may be behind them. If you were fortunate enough to calculate their departure from the "picket line" and be near that position, at that point in time, you could then pass through the line before the other cutters could extend their patrols to overlap the same area. It was an old U-Boat trick from WWII that allowed them to get through the submarine nets, and it worked quite well.

The Department of Defense agreed to my deal. The Department of Justice did not. They would argue this matter for 3 months, while I was sitting in Milan Penitentiary's holding facility in "D" block. Patricia loaded up the kids and went to Monclova, Ohio to stay with Don Thomas (D.T.), and could visit me at the prison. I had to avoid any contact with any of my remaining crew, as I feared that they would get rolled up in this mess. I was relieved that my crew members, still at large, had gone underground. D.T. was returning the favor I had done for all of them back in the day. The mark of a true friend. To this day we are close friends, though we are thousands of miles apart.

Mid-winter arrived, and I was taken to the federal building in Detroit again. It had been awhile, but the government had a counteroffer. It seems that the D.O.D. (Department of Defense) had more pull than the D.O.J. (Department of Justice). The offer was 2 years federal time, and if I would plead guilty to the Michigan State charge then it would run concurrent with my federal charges - and the sentence could not exceed it. My time would be served in federal custody – not state. I could not be charged under RICO statutes, as there had been no activity by me after 1978. The RICO statutes went into effect in 1980. Also under the old sentencing guidelines I could only get 13 years anyway. There was no evidence, and no witnesses to stand up in court against me. Those were the good old days when the accused could confront his accusers. It seems that those who rolled over on me were not ready to take the stand in federal court to face me. Patricia, Paul Borman and I agreed that this was the best solution, and I took the deal.

They transferred me from Milan to a federal holding facility in Washtenaw County, Michigan (Ann Arbor, how ironic). This was only a matter for their convenience. Over the next year I was paraded all over the U.S. to appear in all of the places I landed marijuana, so that all of the local governments and officials could be part of my conviction, and get credit for bringing me to justice. That took about a year and after that Paul Borman got me transferred to a prison camp in the Mojave Desert called Boron. I did my last year there and was released August 4th, 1983.

Patricia had a house all ready for me in San Rafael, California. It was in Lucas Valley. We still had the '30 coupe, our dog, our children and our lives. I went to work as a yacht salesman in Sausalito, and soon learned of the back-stabbing practices of competitive brokers that were fundamental in the trade. I would think of how many people ended up in the trunk of a car, or floating in a canal with a Colombian Necktie for much less, not that long ago. In spite of all this re-adjustment in my life, I still had skills that I could re-adapt and utilize to make a living in this environment that was somewhat foreign to me. I found a niche using my sailing abilities and worked with a broker to sail his customers while he wrote the deals and we split the commission. This allowed me to go sailing everyday, and the brokerage house benefited by my keeping the boats in ship-shape condition. This also allowed me to interact with the owners of the boats, and to do side work for them. This was a very lucrative deal for all the parties involved and it worked for a while, until the owner moved the business to Newport Beach and cut us out of the deal.

I went to work at Nor-Cal yachts as the yard superintendent in Alameda, Ca. That lasted for about a year, until I shattered my right ankle. A cable had let go, and I dropped 30 feet to the deck of a boat that I was rigging. I was hospitalized and in a wheel chair for a year. I had to learn to walk all over again. I started physical therapy and vocational rehab. I was getting a degree in electronics when I came home one day and the house was empty – except for Gypsy, my Doberman. All I had now was my coupe and my dog. It would be 20 years before I found Ryan, Tara, and Erica. I went to pieces and my best friend became cocaine. Everyone had it during those days and even though I wouldn't buy it, my friends thought it was because I could not afford it. So they always came over to my place to party and I would end up with more than I could possibly use.

Rhonda

Years went by, and I drifted around Marin County. I worked as a tow truck driver, and as a mechanic. I even went to school at Mercury Marine training facility in San Leandro, and became certified for Mercury outboards and stern drives. I had various motorcycles, and finally sold the 1930 coupe to Al Silvesteri, a fire investigator from San Francisco. He had been trying to buy it for years, and I knew he would give it a good home.

I put together a basket-case 1982 Harley Sportster. It was fast, and equipped my need for speed. I was living on the edge with no sense of direction, and the bike could possibly provide the solution I may or may not have been looking for. I started hanging out at Trevor's Bar in San Rafael off of 4th street. This bike was a 25th anniversary model, an XL Roadster. The factory forks were 2 inches longer, and it had 3 more degrees in the neck. It was extremely stable at high speeds and I started racing it at night on the street. In a short amount of time I had built up a reputation and there would be a race or two almost every night. There was some serious betting going on and the bartenders were making book off of it. I had my own table, a bar tab, and most of all, friends. I had been enrolled at a bible college in Novato, and was seriously looking for answers as to how to have an intimate one on one relationship with God. I couldn't understand why I had survived so much, and yet I was miserable. What had God created me for in the first place? I knew that God had a sense of humor, but was I some kind of cruel joke?

One Friday in May, at around 5:00 PM I was sitting at my usual table by the fireplace. Only the bartender and I were in there and our conversation consisted of small talk about the racing. That's when my life was about to change.

The front door opened and I don't know if it was the light or what, but I could swear that I saw an angel come walking through the door. She had long, dark brunette hair with glowing hazel eyes. She was wearing a short black leather jacket and Levi's. At 5'5 and a slender build she could not have tipped the scales past 110lbs. We made direct eye contact and both of us were peering deep into each other's souls. There was a clarified sincerity in her eyes that I had never seen in anyone before. She walked up to the bar as I watched her in the mirror that was behind it. I caught her also looking in the mirror back at me. She ordered a drink, and I signaled the bartender to put it on my tab. When she tried to pay for the drink, he pointed to me and said it had been taken care of. She turned around, raised her glass and thanked me, then returned to talking to the bartender.

Robert and Rhonda

I was immediately infatuated with her. I had never ever felt this way before, and something about her moved my spirit in an inspiring way. I couldn't believe it, but I found myself getting up and walking to her. I leaned on the bar next to her and told her that she was the most beautiful girl I had ever seen. She laughed and I thought it was because she had heard that line before. I quickly explained that I had never, ever hit on a girl in a bar and I did not have very good skills. I apologized for my clumsy forward behavior. She said that there was no need to, and politely thanked me for the compliment. I then summoned up the courage to ask her if she might, at some time, go out for dinner with me.

112

Rhonda

She showed me a ring and said she was married. Again I apologized, saying, "That figures, all of the good ones are taken." As I turned away to go and sit down, she grabbed my arm and turned me back to face her and said, "But I am going through the worst divorce from hell."

We talked for a long time as the bar filled up with regulars, and soon it was dark and I had a race. When I returned she was gone, but I could not get her out of my head. At that time a musical group, The Fine Young Cannibals had a song out called, "She drives me crazy," and those words perfectly described what I was experiencing. Over the next couple of weeks we kept running into each other in the strangest places. We were becoming close friends. Her name was Rhonda.

I remember one night at Mike Matzo's place (an out of work bass player of a local bar band), it was too late to travel out of Corte Madera without being stopped by cops. So we all crashed on the floors. Rhonda offered to share a blanket with me and we slept till daybreak. The next morning she got up to cover me with the blanket and to silently depart so as to not awaken anyone else. Instead, I got up with her and as I looked into her eyes I was impressed to see that she was radiantly beautiful without make-up or preparation. She was just naturally beautiful...all of the time. We decided to quietly leave and to go out for breakfast at Zim's restaurant, and then she would go to work.

One night Chuck, Timmy, and I rode to San Francisco on some business for Timmy. I had met these bikers at Trevor's Bar, as they were part of the late night crowd. It wasn't long before we were riding together, if for no other reason than safety in numbers. Our only common interests were our Harleys, riding late at night and the waitresses at the different bars that we frequented between Santa Rosa and San Francisco. We also had mutual ties with old Gypsy-Jokers, the Sons of Hawaii, and Hells Angels out of Oakland and S.F.

On the way back we came into San Rafael and were heading down 3rd street when the traffic light turned yellow. Timmy and Chuck sped through it and I stopped. The next thing I know I was being t-boned by a car out of control. The front bumper struck me right below the knee of my right leg sending me and the bike across the intersection. I was lying in gasoline and this red headed girl of about 18 was screaming "I knew I shouldn't have drank those tequila slammers after taking Valium." She was hysterical. San Rafael police officers soon showed up, and one of

113

them told her to get in her car and leave. He then put a gun to my head and asked where my gun and drugs were.

I said, "What gun, what drugs"?

He asked, "Where is your crank?"

I said, "The bike has electric start."

A lieutenant showed up and asked what was going on. The officer said "I got one of them Hells Angel biker types here."

The lieutenant looked at me and asked, "Duke, is that you?" I nodded yes. The officer was then informed by the lieutenant that I was the recovery tow truck driver that was on 24hr stand-by for vehicles that had gone over the cliffs out on the coast roads.

An ambulance was on its way, and I was taken to Marin General Hospital. They wanted to amputate my leg and I said, "Hell no!" I wanted another opinion.

They shot me full of morphine and insisted that they had to amputate my leg. I refused to sign the consent, and I was finally transferred to the UCSF Medical Center in San Francisco. They took me right in to surgery and started to save my leg.

I awoke the next day and the first person I saw was Rhonda. She was sitting in a chair across from my hospital bed. The nurse said that she had been there for hours waiting for me to come out of surgery. She asked how I was doing and I said, "Fine."

She said, "You better look in the mirror." I was a mess, but the morphine allowed me to muster up some false bravado.

She said that she had heard that her ex-husband and Timmy left me for dead because they had traffic warrants. I said no, it was Chuck and Timmy who left me. That was when she explained that Chuck was her husband that she was divorcing. Until now all Chuck ever commented about his wife was that she was a witch. Then I started to put it all together. I was in love with Chuck's soon to be ex-wife.

Rhonda, laughing, informed me that according to "Biker Code" I could take Chuck's bike, his gun, and his wife. The same was true for Timmy – for leaving me behind. We both laughed. Then the doctors came in to tell me they had just patched me up to stabilize me, and in 72 hours I was going in for the real surgery - where they would put a rod and steel plate in my leg where the bone is missing. For the next two years I would be in and out of surgery, and physical therapy, before I was walking without crutches or a cane. It seems that my right leg was a magnet for disaster.

Rhonda picked me up on my release from U.C.S.F. Hospital, and she took me over to Terra Linda Tow, which was owned by a good friend of ours named Cotton. It was nighttime, and some of our mutual friends were there.

She helped me across the shop, as I was heavily morphined up and on crutches, with a cast that ran from my hip to my toe. Under a cover was my bike. It was still mangled but it was up on its kickstand, and with great difficulty and much encouragement and assistance from Rhonda I crawled onto it. The next thing I knew she crawled over the tank and sat on the bike facing me with her arms around me. She told me to look back over my shoulder and a picture was snapped. I still have that picture to this day. It is one of my favorites. In fact, I have every one of our pictures ever taken.

Robert and Rhonda

One night Rhonda came by my place to pick me up and take me to New George's bar where Arts & Entertainment Television was having an amateur comedy competition. First we stopped at Chevy's bar, she wanted to know what I was like when I got drunk. I explained that I didn't drink alcohol, as I had bad side effects from it. Well, I finally gave in and had a tequila popper. I never had one before, and couldn't even taste it going down. I had another, and then another. We left Chevy's, and then went to Trevor's Bar and I had a few more poppers. Then she noticed the time, and dragged me out of there and off to New George's around the corner. I was feeling pretty good and I signed up for the competition. Next thing I know they called my name.

To get a picture of this let me describe to you what I looked like. I have a cast on my right leg from hip to toe. Rhonda has just put my leather chaps and jacket on me. I am wearing a black bandana and red glass sunglasses – oh yeah – I am on crutches. The crowd started to laugh as soon as I got on stage, which was not easy, as I am now seriously drunk. The M.C. introduced me as, "The Red Eyed Biker from Hell." I had no material ready, so I just winged it as a biker's perspective of the working class civilian. This yuppie values, Porsche driving, mini van soccer mom crowd ate it up. I was able to sarcastically make fun of their idiosyncrasies in a way that allowed them to laugh at themselves. I actually won the competition.

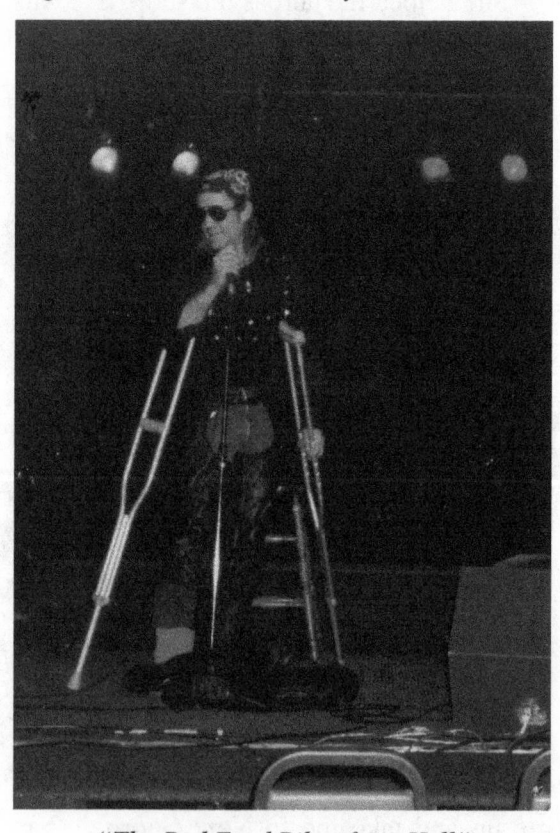

"The Red Eyed Biker from Hell"

After that, Rhonda and I went to the Flat Iron Bar and Grill to celebrate. A friend of ours, Tommy Rox, and his band were playing there. We went on in to the end of the bar, but Rhonda was worried about me as I had not eaten all day. She ran across the street and bought a burrito at the 7-11. She came back and told me to take a bite of it. So I did. I was having trouble biting off a piece and she pulled it back to tear it off. She went to take a bite of the burrito only to find that it had teeth. She broke out in hysterics as my upper denture was stuck in the burrito. She dropped and fell on the floor in the fetal position with tears running out of her eyes gasping for breath between fits of laughter. I picked up my teeth, put them back in and said to the guy staring next to me "What's your fucking problem"? Well when I said the "F" word my teeth flew out again and landed in his mug of beer. Now the bartender was staring in complete disbelief as I grabbed the beer, reached in and got my teeth back again telling the bartender "Give him another beer!" I turned around to see our close friend Carlo picking Rhonda up off the floor. She was in unbridled hysterics and I said, "Let's get the fuck out of here." Again the teeth flew out, sliding across this couples table and landing on a black and white checkered floor. The couple was in shock, I was on my hands and one good knee trying to find my teeth, and Carlo was trying to hold Rhonda up while she was screaming that she was about to piss her pants from laughing. Tommy and his band stopped playing, as they can not believe what they are seeing. We leave the bar, cross the street to the parking lot and get to Rhonda's car - when I go into respiratory arrest - and an ambulance is called to take me to the emergency room.

Rhonda rode with me in the ambulance and I was admitted to the emergency room. The on-call physician happens to be my doctor. He was surprised to see me and asked Rhonda what had happened and she told him. He replied, "Robert can't drink."

And she said, "No shit!"

He then said, "No, I mean Robert can not drink because his system is alcohol intolerant," and he explained to her that I was having a toxic overdose. I was hospitalized and had a violent hangover for a couple of days.

As Rhonda has said many times in her own words, "We're a pair to be reckoned with," and I must admit that she was and still is the compliment that makes me a whole person. For more than 18 years I have never enjoyed life as much as the times that I have shared with her. She has brought out the best in me, and her family has displayed the example of a loving functional unit that I have never known. Because of her I am a better person. I thank God daily for creating her. I thank Him for allowing my life's path to cross hers. And I do believe in miracles.

Rhonda taught me what love really is, she taught me how to love, and even more, she is not only my confidante but she is my best friend. Had I not met her when I did, I would probably not be alive today, as I had lost all faith, all hope, and all interest that this life could offer. Now I seek truth, through accurate knowledge and wisdom in that I may become a better person for her.

Rhonda has been the most positive and influential person in my life.

In 1989 Rhonda and I decided to get a house together. We found one in Petaluma and we moved there with another friend of ours named Kirk. I set up a bike shop in the garage, and when her father had time we would work on all of his military vehicles, or car collection.

During the holidays I would accompany Rhonda to her parents for the family gathering and dinner. Afterwards we would return to our house, and make a dinner for our friends who had dysfunctional families, so as to provide a place for them to escape to. Rhonda has been the most positive and influential person in my life. We have been together through good times and bad times, and those times that we conjointly survived have made us even stronger now. I treasure every minute of it. We started out as very good friends, and the rest has developed one day at a time. We have mutually agreed to disagree on subjects while respecting each others point of view. Rhonda has taught me the true meaning of sincerity and commitment based on mutual respect and admiration. I am now complete as her skills cover my shortcomings. Rhonda is more than a companion, she is a true friend. I only wish that I had met her in the seventies, as her perception of people would have saved me a lot of turmoil and grief.

Summer 1996, Petaluma

While I was sitting on the couch, watching TV, as Rhonda made lunch, a news ad appeared on the screen. It was about a proposition in California called the Compassionate Use Act of 1996. It was to decriminalize marijuana for medicinal use, and eliminate the worry of state prosecution and arrest from the chronically ill patients. It really got my attention, and reminded me of the time in Ann Arbor when we passed the lenient marijuana law through the city council. This was even better because it would be on a *state* level. It stirred memories and emotions within me that had been dormant for years. After all that I had been through, there was now a grassroots movement to bring common sense to law. Not since the repeal of Prohibition (the 18th Amendment being overrode by the 21st Amendment) had there been such an overwhelming collective consciousness to initiate change for the people, by the people. The heart of the people, the pride of California was heard at the polls, and Health and Safety Code 11362.5 became law. The message was clear, and the message was loud. It sent a shudder through the Department of Justice – all the way to Washington D.C., and they did not like it. We shouted compassion – they heard revolution.

About two weeks after the 1st Tuesday of that November I was arrested for 10 marijuana plants in my home that were about 12" tall. I was the first test case in Sonoma County, and maybe even in the state of California. I appeared with a public defender, and the judge turned the case over to a drug diversion program rather than try the case. Andrea Glessner was the director of the drug diversion program and she did background research on me through my doctor, and I was allowed to continue my cannabis therapy as long as I did not test positive for any other drugs.

This relationship continued for a one year period, and we became good friends based on mutual respect. She showed me how to establish a California Public Benefit Non Profit Corporation that would establish my credibility, and non-criminal intent. That was the birth of The Genesis 1:29 Foundation at my home in Petaluma.

To ensure that my efforts were in complete compliance with

California Public Health and Safety Code 11362.5, I decided that it was necessary to establish ties with the State Attorney General's office in Sacramento. Andrea referred me to David DeAlba, who at this time was Assistant Attorney General to Bill Lockyer. A phone call was made, a meeting arranged and off I went to Sacramento.

At first David was unsure as to why I would go to such lengths to establish ties with his office. I informed him that I felt it was much wiser that I should come to see him rather than him coming to look for me. He said that while I was in compliance with California law I was still

Backyard marijuana garden on Bond Ave.

in conflict with federal law. I informed him that I would be responsible for that liability, and under 21 USC 823a. file the necessary applications with the Department of Justice in Washington D.C. (form DEA 225) with an $875 annual payment for an exemption to the Controlled Substances Act.

Now I should be safe to implement paragraph C, "...safe and affordable..." of 11362.5. To regulate how much was being grown, who were the recipients, and a standard of quality control could be documented, and that would then become universal standard. Recuperation of cultivation costs could be justified, and the true beneficiaries would be the patients - with a high quality medicine at a fraction of black-market costs. It was a win-win situation for patients and providers that would set a nationwide standard, and Genesis would be the pioneer grist mill – so to speak.

I cannot tell you in just mere words on paper the feeling that I had in my heart. I was compelled by my conscience, led by my spirituality, and naturally skilled to handle this product in a responsible manner. I had to answer, in the end, to the highest of all authority – God, Himself.

I established Genesis from the 29th verse of the 1st book of the Bible, "For I have given you every herb bearing seed, which is upon the face of

120

all the earth, and every tree, in which is the fruit of a tree yielding seed, to you it shall be for food..."

Genesis operated out of my house at 133 Bond Avenue in Petaluma. In the first couple of weeks we registered over 100 patients. The drug diversion program was referring legitimate patients to us. So did the State Attorney General's office, who described us as a model pilot program. People from all over the state were coming to learn how we established a Public Benefit Non Profit organization, and how to keep patient records, etc.

The secret was that I had brought in help from some of the universities such as Berkeley and Cal Poly. Genesis was a buzz with unbridled creative activity even beyond growing marijuana on location. It was overflowing the capacity of my house, and was becoming a problem in my quiet neighborhood. We were expanding at an accelerated rate, and it had started to deteriorate my relationship with the neighbors. But even more important - It affected my relationship with Rhonda. Her health was not that stable, as she had Crohn's disease, and our home was now invaded by complete strangers. She was displaced by people who she did not even know. The fact is, she did not use cannabis because she did not have compatibility with cannabis therapy. Even the second hand smoke affected her, although she said she enjoyed the smell.

I was blinded by ambition to get Genesis off of the ground, and had somehow put Rhonda on a back burner. I was addressing the needs of complete strangers while taking for granted the person I loved the most. This stress eventually led to her moving into an apartment in a building owned by her father. I was devastated, but, at the same time, obsessed with completing this project. I was torn in two directions. I kept telling myself that if I pushed a little harder, then it would roll on its own with a new generation to run it. I was deceiving myself - and working 20 hours a day.

Rhonda was still looking in on me and she would drag me away to eat lunch, or invite me to her place for dinner and a movie. She was concerned with my weight loss and sunken complexion. It was more than obvious to her that I was deteriorating from being overworked, lack of regular meals and little or no sleep. She said that I was looking like hell, and it saddened her to see me declining into a shell of what she loved. She did not want to be part of me killing myself.

All I could do then was to reassure her that this was temporary, and in just a short while I would be able to retire. I was obsessed with legalizing cannabis federally, and bridging the gap between the state and federal law. I felt that it would purge me of the guilt from all my previous activities in the 70's, and then maybe the faces of death that haunted me in my sleep would finally be put to rest. This only put more pressure on me to accomplish the task at hand. I was a man on a mission, possessed with an obsession to vindicate the remaining guilt buried deep within from the loss of life in Colombia over this plant 25 years before. My perception was clouded and I was in denial, while those who truly cared about me could only look on in desperation.

Robert and Rhonda early days of Genesis 1:29

Establishing Ties in Mendocino

With an increase in patients on a daily basis, the need for more marijuana put stresses on the program. We needed to have an intimate knowledge of the orientation of the cannabis, in that it never crossed a state line, violating the ICC (Interstate Commerce Clause), which would invoke federal authority.

My garage, attic, spare bedroom and back yard were producing the maximum yield per square foot that astounded other growers. We were bursting at the seams, and even the dogs were displaced. We were running out of room to put the trimming, branches and stalks. One night I started to burn the branches and stalks in my fireplace when I got a

I converted the attic into a grow space for marijuana

phone call from David Cormier of the Petaluma Police Department. He asked what I was up to, and I told him I was burning stalks. He told me that they were receiving calls from all over the east side of town complaining about the overwhelming smell of marijuana.

I had no idea that the stalks would carry the smell of burning bud that far, and David ordered me to stop before his supervisor ordered him to respond. People were complaining that I was getting half the town of Petaluma high.

I saw a documentary on hemp and learned there was a man in Mendocino who was making paper from hemp stalks. His name was John Stahl and I immediately contacted him.

Paper made from marijuana plant stalks and stems

John agreed to come down and visit Genesis, as he had also heard about our work. When John arrived, I showed him my abundant supply of material for him to use, and he was amazed at the amount. We immediately entered into an agreement. I would supply him with branches and stalks to produce hemp paper and he would make reproductions of the Declaration of Independence that were accurate down to the *Fleur de lis* watermark. He also became a registered patient along with members of his crew. I helped him to purchase a steam kettle to break down the stalk into cellulose fiber for paper. I was excited because we now had established a chain of custody for all of the plant, which I referred to as whole plant utilization. There was no longer any waste, or leftover from our cultivation.

I explained to John that we had exceeded our ability to generate any increase in the production of cannabis. He suggested that we come up to visit him in Mendocino, and he would introduce me to other members of the community that I may be able to rent some grow space from.

John also informed me that he had an exemption to grow a limited amount of cannabis for research under 21 USC 823a. This was done by filing DEA form 225, filling out the application, and submitting a check for $875 a year. This informed the United States Department of Justice of his activities, and eliminated the suggestion or accusation of a clandestine criminal enterprise. I decided to "Render unto Caesar that which belongs to Caesar" (Mark 12:17) and initiated the foundation to establish a bridge between California patients and the federal government.

Within a month I arranged to meet with John in Mendocino County and to visit his paper mill. I was impressed with the contrast between Mendo and Petaluma. In Legget, old growth redwood trees and primitive land surrounded them. The logging companies had abandoned the area years before, and the economy of the area dissipated - with the decline of jobs equal to the loss of trees. The only redwoods left were on each side of Hwy 101. Any travel east or west of the freeway for more than a mile was wasteland. They left the big trees by the freeway to deter the public outcry of the 70's. The rest they logged out with reckless abandon as to the impact on the environment, community, and most of all the economy. The damages of that era are still seen in the way of scars produced by mudslides, erosions and the overgrowth of blackberries and poison oak. The latter of which are Mother Nature's way of deterring invaders upon her forest.

John introduced me to a man up in Piercy who was about to lose his property. He was in foreclosure, and was years behind in his property taxes. We entered into an agreement to lease his property for a year at a time, pay his back mortgage and take care of his property taxes.

I accomplished this in less than 10 days, and within a month I had a crew up there planting. I leased a tractor and an excavator from Ford New Holland, and the rest is history. It was not long after that more people were approaching me to lease their properties for the same benefits. Our new grow site was up on a cliff overlooking the grounds where the annual Reggae on the River Festival was held. How fitting that a Reggae event was just below an acre of excellent cannabis. We could hear the music as the crew worked in the field. After work the crew went down the cliff to go swimming and enjoy the food and party. This

125

project was so successful that I established another company called Genesis Pharms that would financially stabilize property owners in exchange for cultivation privileges. In one year I had properties from every border of the Emerald Triangle participating to support the implementation of paragraph "C" of California Health and Safety Code 11362.5 - Safe and affordable distribution.

The Democratic Convention, San Jose, 2000

I got a call from John Stahl, and he was telling me that a group of hemp lobbyists were going to the Democratic National Convention in San Jose. They thought that I should accompany them, representing the medical as well as the industrial uses of cannabis. I had never been to one of these events, and my only recollection of one was about the "Chicago 7" (or should I say eight) back in the day in Chicago on August 8th, 1968.

Tom Hayden, Abby Hoffman, Jerry Rubin, Bobby Seale, Rennie Davis, John Froines, David Dellinger, and Lee Weiner organized with some others and disrupted the convention. It made the front covers of both Time and Life magazines.

John and this group were on their way to Petaluma, so I hastily packed my clothes - and for security reasons I made a run to Toys R US. By the time I returned from my errands, members of the group were arriving at my house. I backed the Ford Expedition into the driveway to load it. Some of the group, along with John, decided that it would be better to ride down with me, so as to get better acquainted with each other, and discuss strategies. I was looking forward to an opportunity to meet Congresswoman Maxine Waters. She had impressed me with her defending President Clinton during his impeachment. She had also been Paul Scott's mentor when he opened his Cannabis Dispensary in Inglewood, California, which I supplied with cannabis at harvest time.

Pam, the executive secretary for Genesis, had arranged for 2 suites near the convention hall. When we arrived at the hotel we checked in and quickly went to the San Jose Convention Center to meet with Virginia Strom-Martin and Sam Clauder. Virginia was the Democratic Assembly Woman for Sonoma County. Sam was the Director of "C.A.I.R.", The Campaign for Agricultural and Industrial Renewal, which was at that time trying to re-introduce the industrial and commercial production of hemp and its products. After a round of introductions we were informed that the Democrats, led by Robert Mulholland, were dropping the hemp initiative as a plank in their platform. This would violate our agreement with them, as we had secured a voting base of over 250,000 voters for Al

127

Gore in the California November 2nd election.

Our only option was to collect 250 signatures from the delegates and we had less than 24 hours to do it. We went to work immediately dividing up into teams canvassing the complete convention hall and also the hotels where the delegates were staying. My tactic was approaching older women who could remember the rationing of goods during WWII. I implied that when they run out of toilet paper in the bathroom they may be buying it from Canadians at $5 per roll, as most of our trees had already been cut down, and hemp was a renewable fiber. My campaign was successful enough to register over 70 signatures in a little over 3 hours. By 9 PM that night we had, as a group, collected over 200 signatures, and we decided to resume the next morning.

Most of us retired to our suites at the hotel, and it was not long after that there was an entourage of people coming to the room. Either they could smell the honey oil or they heard about it, but nonetheless the party of the night was at Genesis. I had met a lot of politicians, delegates, and lobbyists who were the movers and shakers of the Democratic Party during our first day there. I was somewhat annoyed at the number of them who enjoyed the "medicinal benefits" of cannabis, but had been reluctant to embrace the efforts to have the plant legalized. I was taken aback of the risk they were taking being in my room. One thing was for certain - everyone enjoyed the honey oil from the vaporizers, because it did not smell like we were smoking pot. We had now become respected colleagues among the elite of politics.

The next morning when we entered the convention center we were met by intense security. A Cuban boy named Elia Gonzales was to be returned to his father in Cuba after his mother had drowned in Florida waters coming to America. Cuban Americans were lobbying to prevent his deportation, and it had become quite a circus. Their tactics were similar to ours, with one unique advantage; they were giving away boxes of Cuban cigars, which were at that time contraband. Meanwhile, our group headed up by John started to collect the remaining signatures and I took off to attempt to gain an audience with Maxine Waters.

I finally found her caucus room in a remote part of the convention hall. I entered the room wearing a black Stetson hat, a black duster, and carrying a large leather briefcase. I was the only white person in there and her security guards were eying me up and down as if I were an assassin sent by the KKK. After her speech I got into the handshake line and progressively moved towards her. I had an ace in the hole, which was a business card that Pamela Byrd's grandmother gave me as an introduction to Maxine. Pamela's grandmother was the head of the Sonoma County Resource Center that also mentored the Sonoma county Drug Diversion Program. Maxine and her had been friends for years and had political ties. When I got up to her I shook her hand, while my left hand pulled her by the elbow closer to me, and I told her "Sonoma County loved her." This was a very risky move on my part considering the environment and my appearance. She felt the business card in her hand that I slipped her during the handshake. She looked at it, again at me and told me to wait for her by the door. I did that directly in spite of her security guards and when she was done with the greeting line she headed out the door and into corridor that leads towards the main caucus room where Al Gore was speaking.

She looked up for me, we made eye contact and then she peeled away and walked directly to me. I introduced myself and she said that she didn't have any time to talk, but if I would "escort an old lady to the main hall" she would listen to me. I agreed and with her on my right arm I escorted her towards the big caucus room. We talked about Paul Scott, his dispensary, cannabis, and AIDS, and The Genesis Foundation.

I used this opportunity to inform her that we donated to the Inglewood, Ca. dispensary around 10 lbs. of clinical grade cannabis a year. I was also trying to ally myself and Genesis with as many congressional and senatorial contacts as possible in order to insure our success in implementing Cal. Health and Safety Code 11362.5. It was important to get feedback and mentoring as we all were navigating in un-chartered waters. I also emphasized to her that this had been a voter initiative with a substantial voting block supporting it. She encouraged me to continue my endeavors and gave me her personal cell phone number with instructions to stay in touch.

When we arrived at the security table in front of the main caucus room we were met by Sam Clauder, Virginia Strom-Martin, John Stahl and the rest of our group. Soon Lynn Woolsey, Barbara Boxer, and others arrived who would be entering the Main Caucus Room to listen to Al Gore's speech. I had to show my ID as I did not have a delegate card to enter. When I set my briefcase down it made a distinctive "klink" sound arousing the suspicion of the security guards - and everyone else for that matter. They immediately wanted me to open it. I said that it was not necessary to take it into the room and I attempted to slide it over to John.

That was not to be the case as they wanted to see what was inside.

All this time John and others had been reassured by me that the brief-case contained everything we needed should we be apprehended by the Secret Service or the FBI and ordered to leave the Convention or be arrested. They had all assumed that the case contained passes, letters of introduction or legal documents. When the security guards opened the briefcase they were shocked along with everyone else, to see that it was full to the top with marbles. Maxine Waters broke out in laughter as she had seen many "Keystone Cops" movies in her day. She looked at me and said, "I like you Robert, you will be very successful, as you swim well with sharks." What she meant was that I could diffuse a dangerous situation with comic relief. One would not need too much imagination to picture Federal Agents trying to chase us while running and slipping on marbles, as we casually exited the building. If nothing else the news would have a field day with the story.

It was at this time I was informed that we had more than enough signatures to have our plank reinstated in the Democratic platform. We then forwarded them to Virginia and Sam to submit to the Democratic Committee. Robert Mulholland was now furious as the powers that be now conceded to honor the agreement if we would not use the words Hemp, Cannabis, Marijuana etc. We challenged him and Susan Pelosi (the daughter of current Speaker of the House Nancy Pelosi) was appointed as our referee. Sam Clauder, John Stahl and I went into a conference room along with Susan Pelosi and some of Mulholland's people. It was getting late and most of the Democrats wanted to get ready for a banquet for Al Gore. We argued semantics for almost an hour when I decided to approach the problem with a bit of wisdom. The name would be changed to the binomial nomenclature of the plant itself. I submitted to replace HEMP with "All Annual Bast Fiber Crops." The proposal was accepted, voted in and passed as a resolution and we were once again still in the game.

The next morning I was sitting with John in the auditorium only to be informed that Robert Mulholland was very unhappy with our success. In
130

fact he was looking for Sam to verbally accost him and to tell all of us to leave the convention. Although I doubted that he had that kind of authority, he did have a certain amount of clout based on his family's financial contributions to the party.

While he may have a considerable amount of influence, he lacked the respect of the real players. They often mentioned that his existence was tolerated out of respect for his grandfather, William Mulholland. The Mulholland influence in the Democratic Party traces all the way back to the 1920's in Los Angeles, California. William constructed the 233-mile long Los Angeles Aqueduct that gave birth to the development of all that L.A. is today. His public life came to a tragic end 15 years later when the St. Francis Dam collapsed, killing over 500 residents of Santa Paula with a 10 story wall of water, and burying the town under 20 feet of mud and debris. Although no criminal charges were brought against him for poor construction, and denying the danger of the leaks reported just hours before the catastrophe, his reputation was destroyed and he withdrew from public life to become a "power behind the throne," so to speak.

I could see Sam and Virginia to my left, when I saw Robert Mulholland coming in from the right. He would pass right in front of me. I told John to stay seated and right when Robert passed in front of me I stood up abruptly and became entangled with him and we were both knocked to the floor by his momentum. I jumped up and got right in his face accusing him of being an inconsiderate scoundrel with no regard or respect to others. As he was fumbling to compose himself and apologize, I walked off giving him a gesture of the back of my hand allowing Virginia and Sam to make a graceful exit out of the room. The situation was now diffused and Mulholland re-attempted his agenda.

At this point in time, I came to the conclusion that I had run out of strategies and I was no longer needed there, as the truly qualified people had that madhouse under control. I proceeded to return home. I had done all that I could do. Sam informed me that there were two seats open in Sonoma County for a delegate, and that I should register for one. I was flattered, but I already had an overwhelming agenda with the growth of Genesis and my research. To sum up the whole event? I made some very good political contacts. I ended with over 20 boxes of exquisite hand-rolled Cuban cigars (the delegates were paranoid of having possession of contraband and gave them to me) as I grew up surrounded by questionable commodities. And I met some wonderful people, such as Virginia and Sam. Last, but not least, I was able to inspect the inner sanctum of our political system first-hand.

Santa Cruz

John called me to see if I was going to Santa Cruz for the Hemp Festival. I had never heard of it before, but he assured me that it was one of the best conventions of hemp products that there was. I felt that it was important for me to learn as much about this plant as I could, now that I was now so involved with it. I would also have an opportunity to meet the people who were the spearhead of the movement attempting to re-introduce hemp as a renewable source of fiber.

I would also have the opportunity to bring the hempacrits and the clinical cannabis rivals together. I called them hempacrits because they claimed to only be interested in cannabis for its industrial and commercial value, although they would be smoking it in the closet, so to speak. All the while denying their recreational, and/or clinical use of cannabis.

Things were running smooth at Genesis, so I felt that I could be spared for a couple of days, and I agreed to go. We loaded the Expedition and headed down the road for Santa Cruz. On the way John was able to bring me up to speed about the festival and the players. By the time we arrived the event was well underway. John had previously reserved a booth for us, and we set up our displays immediately. He had a variety of paper products there, and I had brochures about The Genesis Foundation. John introduced me to a lot of people there, such as Mikki Norris and Chris Conrad, then I met Jack Herer. Later that afternoon I was privileged to meet the maker of hemp US flags. I outlined our operation to him and I explained that we were setting up cottage industries that were making medicine and products from cannabis. We were not importing hemp, we were in fact growing it and producing fiber while manufacturing usable goods. This was whole plant utilization.

I was impressed with Tim's American flags. He even produced a 13 star "Betsy Ross" version which I liked the best. It just shouted old school at you when hemp was the only fiber crop in America, before the British introduced cotton in the south. His flags were a compliment to John's Declarations of Independence that were printed on hemp paper, produced from my stalks. Tim was somewhat of a loner who really didn't fit in with any particular group. Yet he felt a common ground with John and I, as we were cut from a similar stalk. All three of us were outcasts who had made it through life on our own merit, yet we recognized that regarding cannabis, we were all three on the same page.

That evening we were invited to a, "Bud and Breakfast Hotel," that was a meticulously restored Victorian home in Santa Cruz. I went with two vaporizers, a ¼ lb of bodacious bud and an ounce of pure honey oil. We set up the vaporizers and in a short period of time two lines were formed to try the oil in the vaporizer. The air was permeated with the smell of fresh bud during harvest time. It was the perfume of the fruit of the vine, unlike the usual smell of burning vegetable matter. All of the people who took advantage of this unique opportunity settled back into small groups of enlightening discussion, which lasted through till the wee hours of the morning.

Peace and harmony were abundant, and for the rest of the festival most conversations reverted back to that evening. The proprietors of the Bud and Breakfast gave me the finest compliment when they informed me of all of the pleasant comments that were made of their house and the honey oil event. I was truly moved and I could see the start of something that I so much wanted to continue. I felt that while cannabis may not be able to save the world, it could improve it.

The VAN Hotel

When I would travel up through Mendocino I would always go through the town of Willits and pass the Van Hotel. This was a four-story hotel made of brick and stone left over from the Boom Days longs gone by. It was the centerpiece of the town. It was also empty. The Victorian Bud and Breakfast had given me an idea and I wanted to do the same with the Van, only on a larger scale. It could have hemp product shops on the main floor, with a restaurant, a bar and maybe even a museum. I had been researching the cafe scene of Amsterdam and I felt that this redevelopment of the Van would generate an economic boom for the whole town of Willits and Mendocino County as well.

So when the festival was over in Santa Cruz we packed up the Expedition and, along with a few more people who had joined us, we proceeded north, not to Petaluma but on to Willits. My idea had generated some interest from other vendors who were interested in having shops that were open daily instead of just a few festivals or conventions a year.

We spent two days in Willits and met with local businessmen and members of the City Council in non-official capacities to discuss the project. We needed feedback as to whether there would be community support or possibly resentment. You must understand that small communities are skeptical of outside entrepreneurs all of a sudden taking an interest in their town. They had been previously exploited and then abandoned by the logging companies, which led to the shut down of the lumber mills, trucking, and subsequently many of the restaurants and the motel/hotel businesses. The place was left devastated in many ways. We needed to establish, right from the beginning, that we were not intending to exploit their community, but rather, proposed a Mutual Benefit endeavor. It was our intention to use all the local contractors, work force and planners. This would create a win-win situation for us and the townspeople that was economical as well as political.

Willits was in a remote area and it was cheaper to use the local talent and infrastructure that was already in place. We had no intention of bringing in outside vendors or consultants unless it was absolutely apparent that the needs for the demand could not be met locally.

The response was overwhelmingly supportive and the buzz in town was about the possibility of this project going forward. We made arrangements to contact the owner of the building who lived in Sacramento. This would be the latchkey to the whole project getting off the ground.

The owner was an older Greek gentleman who had inherited the building. At first he was entertaining the option of selling the building, but he was reluctant to arrange a face-to-face meeting. Peculiarly, the more that we pressed him for this meeting, the more distant he became. I had no intention of initiating a project of this capacity through independent mediators who would probably be attempting to profit from a commission or insisting on a partnership. The only partners I was interested in would be those who shared the same interest in the commerce and promotion of cannabis and would be sharing in the same financial liability.

After many months of hard work to put this deal together we all arrived at the same conclusion. The owner of the Van was interested in the failure of the local businesses and the town of Willits as a whole. These sentiments were expressed by him verbally in direct phone conversations that I had with him. I never discovered whether this was personal or sentimental, but it was definitely financial. I can only assume that if Willits failed as a town then there would be substantial real estate opportunities for him and any other financial investors who could purchase the remaining businesses and properties for pennies on the dollar.

This was not anything new, nor unique, but was a common corporate business tactic. This practice is sometimes referred to as a hostile takeover. Even though it may be subtle, and over a long period of time, the results are the same. I had seen this happen many times before, years ago, in Colombia, South America.

Patients, Pills, People

With the Van Hotel project laid to rest I was back and focused on my research and patient load. I had recently met Charlie Coco who was working for Centaur Pharmaceutical Company. He had contacted me after learning about the Genesis Foundation on our website. We made arrangements for him to visit the facility on a weekend, as he was very interested in my ability to isolate the THC molecule which we had talked about in length. He said that his first exposure to the honey oil was in Ann Arbor Michigan in the early 70's and no one had seen the original oil since. There were only counterfeit knock offs of what was the real thing and they were disgusting.

When Charlie arrived he had a surprise for me. He brought a rotovaporator with him. This would speed up the process of making some of the oil by separating it from the reagent rapidly. Then the reagent could be measured to confirm that what was left was pure oil.

We set it up in the garage and started the process. He hadn't brought any accessory equipment for the rotovap so I made an ice cooler and a pump into a coolant circulator with some rubber hose, water and dry ice.

Charlie was really impressed with my "Rube Goldberg" approach to laboratory work, and it was not long until we looked like a couple of kids locked in a candy store. He jokingly made a comment that if we only had a vacuum pump for a few inches of vacuum we could make the oil in a continuous loop cycle. I looked him right in the eye and said: "Oh, yeah? no problem."

In a remote corner of the garage I pulled out a manual vacuum tank from a M.A.S.H. unit that dated back to the Korean war. Rhonda had gotten a shipment of artifacts for her military antique store and this was part of the lot. They had no use for it and for some reason she felt that I could use it. It sat around for over two years and now I knew why I ended up with it. Fate! Charlie was flabbergasted and jokingly asked if there was anything I didn't have stashed somewhere.

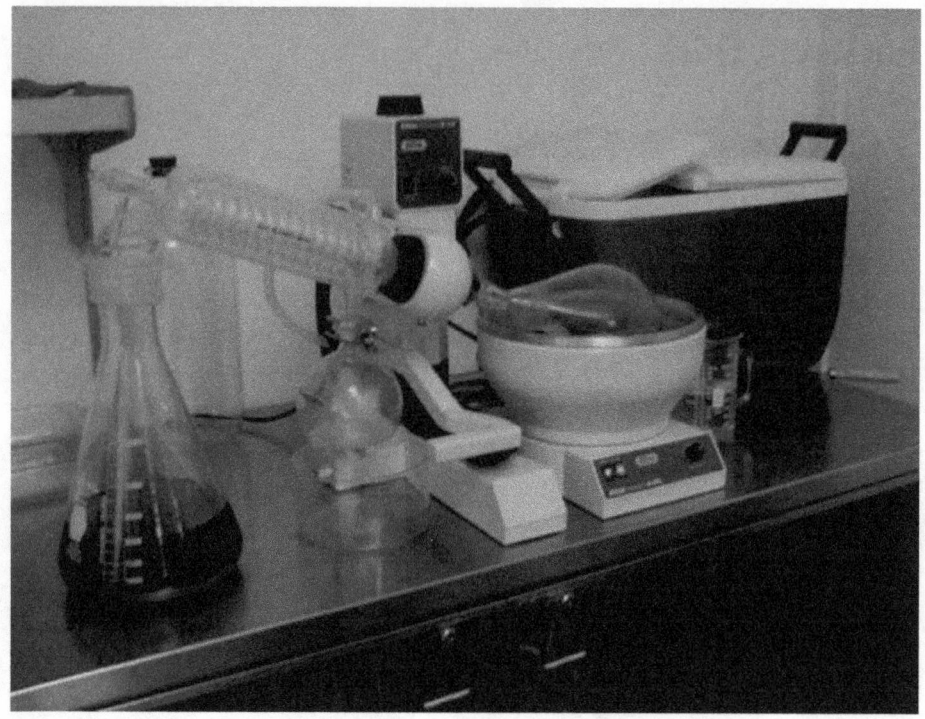

Making "Honey Oil" with a "Roto-Vap"

Charlie's position with the pharmaceutical company was to write research protocols. When we sampled the product we had just isolated, we agreed to form an alliance and push this product through FDA testing, and phase 3 clinical trials as soon as possible. To do this we needed a research protocol, which was agreed to be equal in value to the product I made. We conceded that we had nothing as individuals because the product needed the research protocol and vice versa. A 50/50 split was our agreement. We shook hands and I immediately phoned Bill Hyde who was not only a good friend of mine, but more important, a patent attorney.

While Charlie was back home writing the protocol, I purchased a new *Büchi* R-114 rotovaporator, and started producing large amounts of oil for testing. At the same time Bill was filing our patent applications, and in a short period of time we were issued patent pending file numbers. We were on the road to establishing medicinal values for cannabis. About a week later I was graced by the appearance of Dr. Tod Mikuriya, who had heard about my honey oil, and wanted to examine it in order to make sure of its quality. He came right out and said that he had seen other oils that he referred to as glorified crankcase oil, and had warned people to avoid the use of them.

I showed him the complete process and he was relieved to see the professional, clinical and meticulous care that was incorporated into the manufacturing of the oil. This included accurate record keeping, chain of custody and inventory control for each batch. When he sampled the oil in my vaporizer, he was thoroughly impressed, and endorsed my product without reservation. This was the start of a bond between Dr. Tod and me (and Genesis) that was based on mutual admiration and respect. Little did I know then that this would prove to be a solemn asset for the both of us when the Feds started their witch hunt.

During this time I meet Dylan Katz and his mother. Dylan was well known from the media coverage of his being beaten half to death and suspended in a coma for over 3 months. This started when his grandmother bought him a 49er's football jacket, which he proudly wore to school. Because of gang violence and activity in Santa Rosa, he was approached and ordered to take off the jacket. He refused. What ensued was the beating of his life, which left him in a coma with severe neurological damage. For a while doctors doubted whether he would live. Then, they were not sure if he would come out of the coma, and if he did, their guess was that he would be paralyzed. That was not to be the case, Dylan had other plans!

I awoke early one morning to the barking of the dogs. Someone was knocking at my front door and it was barely light. I saw a woman at the peep-hole and so I opened the door to see this young emaciated teenager slumped in a wheelchair and a mother, pale in complexion with the eyes of hopelessness. The woman asked if she was at the right address, and if I was Robert Schmidt. I answered her question and invited them in inquiring as to what I could possibly do for them. That is how and when I met Dylan Katz. I was curious as to why they were looking for me.

Dylan's mom got right to the point. She had been through a barrage of doctors, neurosurgeons and the like. With all of the marvels of modern medicine they were at the end of their hope for Dylan. That is until one of the doctors suggested taking him to Genesis to see me.

Their prognosis of Dylan was based upon nerve damage suffered during his attack. This trauma was not surgically repairable, and it limited his ability to sit up, move and/or walk - due to lack of neuromuscular control. He was in pain, but when I talked to him, though his speech was slurred, he conveyed to me that he had not given up.

My first concern was to alleviate as much of his pain as possible. I discussed different cannabis therapies that were available, so that considering her intimate knowledge of Dylan we could initiate a program for him. I showed her a vaporizer, and suggested we try it for immediate pain relief in order to stabilize him. She agreed, and I showed her how to operate it. I went off to finish getting dressed, as the Genesis crew would be showing up for work very soon.

When Pam and Barry, our Receptionist and Dispenser, came in, I introduced them to Dylan and his mother, and I saw Pam's eyes water up as she was holding back her tears. They all knew of Dylan from TV news, and he immediately became a celebrity with us. Even the dogs liked him, as I could not get Dakota (my Australian shepherd) to leave his side. She kept sneaking back into the house to sit in front of him. Pam registered Dylan as a patient, and Barry prepared a package of edibles, honey oil, buds, a vaporizer, a t-shirt and more for them. There would be no charge for our services as we put Dylan in our research group. I could write off the loss, and his high profile case could not be disputed if there was a medical challenge by the D.E.A.

When I had returned to the office from getting dressed, I was amazed to see that Dylan was sitting up in his wheelchair, and he was talking to Pam, Barry and other members of the crew. This showed that he was responding to the THC therapy positively, so I started to select buds for him from the indica strain, as they have the opposite effect of the sativa strain, which is a relaxer. Dylan needed stimulation. He had been dormant in the coma for too long, and we needed to wake up his neuromuscular activity.

Over the next couple of weeks Dylan's mother would come by to pick up his medicine and brief us on his progress. The therapy was also having a positive effect on her, as I could see a change in her appearance. She was talkative, positive, and no longer had that sunken complexion of despair that only a loving mother without hope would have. She was so grateful for all that we were doing for her son, and we were grateful for the opportunity. Dylan's progress reports from his doctors only inspired us to further our work. Whenever we got tired, or just frustrated, we would think of Dylan, and imagine trading places with him. That thought alone renewed our energy.

It was 3 months since I met Dylan when there was a knock at our door. In front of us, on crutches, was Dylan. He was no longer in a wheelchair, and in fact he was there with his girlfriend who had driven him over to us. We were all in shock, and there was an atmosphere of pure joy in the room. The crew all stopped their work (including Dakota) to come up to him and just touch him in disbelief. He looked really well, and he told us that his doctors were astonished at his progress. In not too many weeks after that he only needed a cane. He was doing well in physical therapy, and at the time of my arrest he was just as solid as most boys his age, other than the scars he had from his surgeries.

We had now developed a process of binding the honey oil to echinacea, ginkgo biloba and other herbs so as to be able to encapsulate the THC in a pill dosage form. We were struggling with the dosages. Our test base consisted of 100 patients who volunteered for the program. The candidates were selected and formed into groups based on their ailment, age, weight, and gender. They had to agree not to smoke marijuana or use any other pain suppressants. Genesis would supply them with the capsules that were made specifically for them.

Chelsea was an employee who assisted in the gardening of the cannabis, trimming, and production of the honey oil. Pam and Chelsea were in charge of encapsulating the pills in the lab under specific guidelines. Batches were made in specific numbers and logged into a control book, recording the exact amount of THC oil per 100 pills, the date, and the binder that was used. We were very strict about this work, and it was done in the lab without interference or interruption. Quality control was our main concern, as we needed to know how to regulate and dispense accurate dosages in pill form. We were setting a guideline for our research protocol.

One evening Chelsea and Pam asked me if they could make up some pills for their own use to relieve their menstrual cramps. I reluctantly agreed, on the condition that they recorded exactly what they were doing in the control log. No problem, or so I thought. This was on a Friday night.

141

When Monday came around Chelsea did not show up for work 'till noon. Pam came in about 3. Both of them were being very quiet, but went about their work. I could not help but notice that they were quietly having a serious conversation in the lab as they worked. When 5pm came around, I came in with a vaporizer and started to load it up. I asked them where they had been on Saturday, as they had been scheduled to work. They looked at me and started to laugh. I asked what was so funny, and Chelsea told me that she didn't even remember Saturday, or Sunday and just woke up on Monday. Pam then asked me not to get mad, and she would explain.

Both of them told me this story of making some pills for themselves. I immediately reached for the control log but Pam's hand was quicker. She held it to her chest with both arms around it and reminded me of my agreement. I acknowledged and she handed me the logbook opened to the last entry. It turns out that the girls had raised the dosage beyond our highest percentage by 400%! I went berserk inside, and I was really struggling with the liability to our credibility for such an irresponsible action. I used the vaporizer for a pause to regain my composure as it was very important as to how I would deal with this and I needed time to think it through. It was obvious that they were OK. I needed to document the result of such an overdose. I set the vaporizer down and asked them to fill in the logbook under results. Pam said they wanted to but were having trouble describing in clinical terms for, "imagine being paralyzed and waking up in a motel room, stark naked with a smile on your face from ear to ear, and not caring."

Chelsea agreed.

I sat down silently in shock and disbelief of what I just heard. I grabbed the vaporizer, took a long draw, paused, exhaled and reminded them of our responsibility to all of the patients who depended on us. They assured me it would never happen again, and then I started to laugh.

Home Invasion

Gary Kubeck was not only an employee of Genesis working for me, but he was also living at my house. We were working two shifts a day to keep the growing production up and the lab work done. Gary, at the time, was separated from his wife, and I let him sleep on the couch, in the front room/office. On weekends his children, 11-year-old Greg and 9-year-old Michelle, would stay with him at the house, and would camp out in front of the fireplace in sleeping bags. I enjoyed the company of Greg and Michelle, and they treated me as if I was their uncle. Sid was my partner in the Genesis Project and at that time he was the president of the corporation as I was the Founder. He would occasionally stay at my house as he was on the road or up north most of the time. We had all known each other for years.

One evening while I was sitting up in bed, going through our paperwork with the TV on in the background, I heard some loud activity in the front room. I thought that the dogs were outside, but with the kids there you just never knew. They were always playing with them.

Then out of the corner of my right eye I saw Sid backing into my room along with Gary and Greg. Their arms were in the air.

Next I saw Michelle backing into the room, and someone had her by the hair and a gun pointed in her face. I rolled out of bed to the right and onto the floor, jumping up between Michelle and the gunman - separating them. The gun barrel was now up against my forehead, and I was looking into the eyes of the gunman. I thought the gun was a 45 caliber Colt automatic. I pushed forward and kept my head pressed hard against the barrel (A Colt 45 has a safety device incorporated in the design to prevent the gun from exploding. It will not fire if there is pressure on the end of the barrel). I continued to stare down the gunman while giving orders to Gary to put the kids in the bathtub and get on top of them.

I yelled at Sid that when I take the gun he must come over the top of me and secure it in case it flies away. "No matter what happens to me do exactly as I say. We are not giving them control here." The gunman was threatening to blow my head off. He had a glove on, so I could not see when his fingernail darkened, to be able to tell when he was squeezing the trigger. All I could do was to keep staring in his eyes for that signal, that only his eyes would make, to let me know that he was pulling the trigger.

Shouting and threatening sounded through the air and my eyes were getting dry. I could not afford to blink. I might miss the signal that I was looking for or even worse, trigger his reflex. Finally he blinked and my right hand shot straight up to the gun forcing it into the air.

I rolled to the ground with the gunman and we scrambled in the hallway. Sid could not get past. The accomplice, upon seeing all of this, bolted for the front door, and the gunman went scurrying on all fours following behind him. That was when Gary grabbed the gun and showed me that the gun was not a Colt 45, but rather it was a Glock 17, which did not have the safety device I based my strategy on! Sid took off out the front door chasing after them. We could not call 911 because the invaders had cut our phone wires. Sid called the police on his cell phone. They responded quickly and caught the accomplice immediately. The gunman though, was still at large. Sid had noticed a strange car in the neighborhood, and when he looked in through the windshield he saw a box for the Glock handgun on the front seat. The accomplice had a set of keys on him that matched the car, so the gunman was still hiding somewhere in the neighborhood. We organized with the police and started a search for him. At daybreak Sid found him hiding in a drainage ditch, signaled the Petaluma police and the gunman was captured and taken into custody.

At his trial Judge Passalacqua gave him 104 years in State prison for armed assault, attempted armed robbery, kidnapping, and more. It was a victory for us in that the police assisted us instead of prosecuting us. It was a success in that a message was sent loud and clear to criminals that growers and patients were no longer easy targets that had to remain silent for fear of going to jail for cannabis cultivation. It was a success because justice prevailed. It also meant that Genesis had outgrown my house, and I needed to move the dispensary and lab into a commercial area. It was like I was at work 24 hours a day, 7 days a week, never leaving. I was being consumed by it and there was no relief.

Truthfully speaking though, I can only thank God that Rhonda was safe in her own apartment across town, and did not have to endure such a horrific experience. Nonetheless she read me the riot act about jeopardizing the safety and lives of Michelle and Greg, whom she loved very much like her own. Things needed to change.

The Debate

One morning after the trial, I received a phone call one morning from David Jacks of the Northern Lights church. He had an associate in L.A. who was an officer in the L.A. Stage Hands Union. They were hoping, or more like insisting, that I fly to L.A. and attend this debate. A guy named Andy Kinnon would pick me up and deliver me to the Ronald Reagan Library of Law at Chapman University in Palisades, Ca. The Drug Czar, Barry McCaffrey was addressing a conference there and attacking Proposition 215, or actually California Public Health and Safety Code 11362.5. David and Andy felt that my research, my registrations, and my self-esteem were what would be needed to challenge the lies perpetrated by the Federal Government to suppress cannabis research and clinical development.

I must admit that while I was flattered, I felt like I was crawling into a lion's den covered in meat sauce. They assured me that there would be a number of students there and I would not be without support. Reluctantly, I agreed to do the deed. The conference would be that afternoon and they had already arranged a plane reservation for me.

I put on my double-breasted dark blue power suit, packed my briefcase and set off for the airport. This was one trip where no member of my crew asked to go with me. I really did not blame them, and jokingly praised them for their common sense. As for me, I felt like I was approaching an angry father with a bad report card and a note from my teacher.

I was met at the airport by Andy, who was holding a sign with my name on it, and he led me away to a white Lincoln. It was an executive limo of modest size, but did have a divider window and rear facing seats. Andy began to brief me and supply background information on Chapman University, its significance and the nature of this conference. Chapman is a private university for the upper crust of American families. It is not your scholastic achievement that grants you access, rather it is your pedigree. Most of the students there were the offspring of politicians or captains of industry. The point here is that this school was a safe haven for the elite of America who regulate, lobby, or initiate the political environment and standards of America, including its foreign policies.

We arrived at the University and quickly proceeded to the Ronald Reagan Library of Law. There was a conference room there, and this dog and pony show was about to get underway. Andy had a table reserved for me, and I was instructed to feel under the table to find where a microphone had been taped. The program was to have General McCaffrey make his speech about the increase of drug abuse in America, and then a presentation of statistics with pictures, graphs, and paraphernalia. That would be followed by a question and answer period for members of the audience. That would be my cue.

During Barry's presentation I took notes and with my calculator I was crunching his numbers. I noticed a pattern immediately and it became the foundation of a blueprint to expose the deception perpetuated by NIDA, the DEA funded by pharmaceutical companies, and the DuPont dynasty. The billboards for this event listed these as the sponsors of the conference in the bottom right hand corner in one-inch letters.

When the question and answer period of the program started, I raised my hand, and waited patiently for my turn to be called on. Finally my turn came and I reached under the table, grabbed the mike and stood up in full view of those in the room. Now Barry's composure changed quickly and I addressed him with this question, "General McCaffrey, after listening to your statistics am I to understand that the average marijuana plant confiscated by the DEA is over eleven feet tall and produces 3.8 pounds of marijuana that sells for over $8,000 per pound?" Then I held up the piece of paper with his statistics on it and challenged him to crunch his own numbers.

I then turned to the crowd, which was the cue for the soundman to raise the volume on my microphone and lower the sound at the podium. I looked at the parents and the students and explained to them that if you perpetrate a lie and you are the only one believing it, then the only one being deceived is yourself. If parents tell their children that smoking marijuana will destroy their chromosomes and lead to birth defects, that smoking marijuana will destroy their brain cells, that smoking marijuana will lead to craving hard drugs like heroin, or that smoking marijuana inspires violent activity in the user, what then happens when their children smoke it and discover that none of this is true? You leave them no other conclusion than that you are stupid, naïve, or a patholgical liar.

148

At a minimum, it will sever any trust or bond that you may still have with your children. Furthermore, why would they still believe in the dangers of cocaine or heroin use? Then I asked the students whether or not what I said was true, and emphasized my point by directing the microphone to them in a sweep around the room. There was unanimous agreement that thundered the room. At this point Barry McCaffrey stomped off the stage with his entourage of security guards.

At that point I introduced myself by name and title as the founder of Genesis 1:29 Foundation of Sonoma County. I gave a brief description of our work and how patients were benefiting from clinical cannabis. I was not prepared for such a positive response - especially from the parents. I lacked the material to continue my oration for more than 15 minutes. I was talking from the heart, without notes, describing cottage industries growing out of this movement. I talked about 60,000 new jobs in California in the first year. I talked about the possibility and merits of a tax base that could be directed specifically for the reconstruction of our education systems and after school programs.

I mentioned that since cannabis had been labeled as the "Assassin of Youth," we should let the revenue from its tax base rebuild its infrastructure. At that last comment I thanked them for their time and attention, set down the microphone, picked up my briefcase and headed for the door. What happened next was so amazing that I am still confounded by it even today.

As I was walking down the hall to exit the building I was literally mobbed by students, parents, doctors, professors, etc. They were patting me on the back, grabbing my arm to shake it, handing me business cards. In turn, I was handing out mission statements, and my business cards, but I was running out of them quickly, and that is when I started to panic. I am not used to crowds, and this was way too intense for me. Then my cell phone rang and it was Andy. I told him that I was freaking out, and he told me to stay calm and keep walking toward the car. Whatever I do, do not stop walking towards the car. He and some of his crew had the car waiting for me and in a few seconds they would open a path for me to make it into the car. Soon I saw Andy in the Lincoln with the door open waiving me towards him. I got in the car and I was shaking violently. He said that this often happens to celebrities, and he and his crew were experienced at handling crowds. The driver sped us off and I lit up a joint – a big fat one soaked in honey oil. My heart was pounding through my chest, but Andy and his crew were laughing and joking to me that I had better get used to this if I was going to continue with my current endeavors to expose the truth about cannabis.

I told them that I would be all right when I got on the plane. They looked at each other with comical expressions and told me my flight home had been canceled, as I was going to attend a dinner party near Malibu at an exclusive residence. They said I was the celebrated guest, and that the host had insisted on my presence. I objected, as I had not made arrangements for such an extended visit, but Andy assured me that I could be on a later flight that night, and it would be beneficial to Genesis if I complied with this request for my appearance.

We went to Andy's house to chill out until the party, as he needed to change clothes for the event. I was able to meet his family and members of the Los Angeles cannabis coalition. At this time, they had been enduring extreme oppression of the opening of cannabis clubs in Southern California. The environment was drastically different from San Francisco, Sonoma, Mendocino and Humboldt. I was immediately humbled and found a new appreciation for the attitude of our politicians, law enforcement officers, and the public in general. Our communities were at least open to allowing pilot programs to get off the ground, and willing to make adjustments to them that would assist them in integrating positively into their communities. Even though there was extreme division of opinion regarding the cannabis clubs or dispensaries, many were open, and providing a functional service in their communities.

I thought Andy was a family man who was focused on his children and his wife. All of his other interests were required to be second in priority after his family interests had been served. I was impressed. I could see the positive attitude and the loving and respectful response displayed by his children. It was an enjoyable time. The Lincoln returned, and it was time for us to go off towards Malibu. Andy and others were briefing me on what would be happening at this party. It would start with a cocktail party made up of the elite of L.A. politicians, doctors, judges, and some celebrities. We could not use cannabis there, but the host was a patient, and had made provisions for self-medication (smoking a bud).

We entered a gated community complete with a guardhouse and

armed security. As we approached the house I could see the sun setting on the horizon of the Pacific Ocean behind it. It was radiantly red and created a mirror image on the horizon that resembled a figure 8 for a short period of time. I thought of it as a good omen. Ship captains say: "Red at night, sailor's delight," and I was about to navigate through some unfamiliar waters at this event. I was introduced by a doorman upon entering the house. The atmosphere of this environment was permeated with the smell of old money and bloodlines. Everybody was a somebody, and they carried themselves in posture and speech that one would expect from those with an air of superiority. I was totally out of my element here, but as I had been previously briefed that I was an invited guest, I carried on. I took notice of faces that were familiar from the previous activities of that afternoon at the university, and as these individuals approached me I was re-introduced to them, and then introduced to their friends, and colleagues. I had a glass of *Cabernet Sauvignon* in my left hand while I shook hands with my right.

While I was making small talk with all of these new introductions, my mind was trying to figure out how to get some of those jumbo prawns being carried around on silver platters by waiters. I only had two hands and I was hungry. I made my way over to a serving bar and made a small plate of an assortment of the many *hors d'ouvres* that were prepared and artistically displayed in patterns amid ice sculptures. As I was enjoying the prawn cocktail and lobster bits, the host came up to me and inquired as to my need for anything, and what I thought of the affair. I made a complimentary comment, and it was followed by the opportunity to take a break and get away for a moment.

Now Andy, our host and I were heading outside to the balcony that hung over the cliff. We exited through a gate that led to a brick staircase, that windingly led down to the beach. We crossed the beach and walked south to a picnic table where we all sat down. I needed to catch my breath. I reached inside my blazer and pulled out a bag of buds - and from my watch pocket I pulled out a vial of honey oil. Our host's eyes lit up, and he asked if that was the oil everyone was talking about. I said I think so, and I let him smell the vial. He was stunned by the smell of the oil. He described it like a vintner appraising a rare vintage wine for its clarity, bouquet, the palatability. I was impressed by his admission. My product was getting its due adulation at last.

151

While we were sitting there smoking this honey oil saturated joint, he inquired as to whether or not I recognized this place. I told him that I didn't remember ever being in this area before. Then I looked at the picnic table, sliding my hand over it. Yes, there was something very familiar, yet vague, about this place. I had in fact, been there before. He mentioned casually that he would expect that, as it was more than 20 years since I had been there.

"Who are you?" I inquired. He smiled, Andy looked puzzled and our host began to tell me that I had been there with Patricia and Ryan a few days before I was arrested. I was on my way to Mexico and I had met with my mother so that she could meet her grandson. I was driving a 1930 Model A Ford coupe.

I was now in a state of shock, as he continued to explain that my grandfather was a 33rd degree Mason knighted in Scotland. I was the son of both houses: the house of Herold, and my father's family Schmidt, who were land owners back on the island of Put-in-Bay. Captains of industry had estates on the island before the 1900's. U.S. Presidents would summer there at the Hotel Victory until it burned down in 1919, and then they used Camp David. Powerful members of the Freemasons had property there, and it had become their stronghold and reserve, as the island was made of solid bedrock. My grandfather was a powerful Mason who had no sons, and my mother was a daughter of the Eastern Star. My older half-brother Larry was from my mother's first marriage, and I and my sister were from her second marriage. The point I need to make here is that a complete stranger was telling me facts about my family that even I didn't know about. Someone or something had been monitoring my life since I was a child! It turns out that my own mother gave the authorities my whereabouts, which led to my being apprehended in Stockton years ago. After my arrest my mother was able to give my grandfather's Masonic ring to Larry without any reservation or dispute, and he would be the heir to whatever accompanied it, and a legacy would continue.

I looked at Andy, he looked at me and we finished the joint in silence. Not long after that, we headed for the airport. It was an interesting ride. We didn't talk a lot, but what we did talk about was important. We were trying to figure how all of this was relative to our current endeavors to legalize marijuana. Would it work for us or would it work against us?

The New Offices and the Circle Star Ranch

Genesis had exceeded not only the capacity of the house, but the neighborhood too. We were becoming a nightmare to the other residents that stemmed from the constant traffic, parking and - most of all - the home invasion. Bond Avenue was no longer a peaceful suburban community; it was a bustling den of activity. My landlord had been receiving complaints, and he was forwarding them to me. While he was supportive of my work, it was becoming more of a problem than he needed to deal with.

We had been working with a ReMax realtor for more than a year, but as yet, we were no closer to closing a deal than when we started. Maybe a rental or lease was not as profitable as the sale of a property, and that could be a significant incentive for a real estate agent.

My chief financial officer, Carlos, located office spaces near the DMV in Petaluma. They were upstairs, but they were available. We would gladly deliver to any patients who could not make the climb. We signed the lease just in time to head off our official eviction notice. We completed the move and set up Genesis in less than 72 hours, even transferring the phone numbers to the new location.

It was a breath of fresh air, but I still needed another residence with enough room for cultivation. In the meantime I would stay with my friend Tom Umphries at his house, as he was going through a divorce. Rhonda's apartment was no more than a studio, and it was in no way large enough for me and the dogs and my belongings. This period though, did allow us to spend some time together having dinner and watching TV.

It took about a month but we found a ranch in Sebastopol, California. It bordered the Ragle Regional Park and was at the dead end of Martin Lane off of Mill Station Road. It was a landmark property that was the original ranch/farm in that area for over a hundred years before, which had been owned by the Martins, a family who pioneered the town of Sebastopol. It had 17 acres of land and a few outbuildings.

Marijuana garden at Circle Star Ranch in Sebastopol, Northern California

We leased the property with an option to buy in the event that my honey oil patents were successful. We were gambling on our efforts to bring some common sense and medical validity to clinical cannabis. The whole enchilada would be on the line this season.

The property needed some work to come up to farming and ranching standards. I had a crew that was more than capable, and also the equipment to farm it. I made Jeremy my ranch foreman, as he had grown up on a farm in Oregon, and could operate the tractor, and accessory equipment, without losing any body parts. I was concerned with safety, as we had taken the Genesis Project to another level, and I could remember what some of these guys had done in the past.

Our public relations officer and webmaster, Steve DeLaney, had arranged for Noel Cisneros of KRON TV4 to film our trimming of a large harvest from Yreka. I had a remote piece of property hidden between Sebastopol and Petaluma with two huge overseas cargo containers on it. They were for drying and trimming the harvested bud. I met Jeremy and his girlfriend Hope during the harvest, and they came south with the load to became part of our crew. Hope was working at the dispensary as a receptionist.

We took Noel and her film crew to the area in a roundabout way, so as to confuse its location. We gave them the "money shot" of two cargo containers full of marijuana. They were allowed complete freedom of mobility and filming. This was the most marijuana they had ever seen, and they gave us a positive slant on our efforts, as they interviewed each and every one of the trimmers. It was a pleasant experience for both parties, and when it was aired on TV the commentary was positive. I think that this interview was a milestone event, as most of the news about cannabis was in reference to raids by law enforcement, and a negative overtone would prevail. This one was about the implementation of California Health and Safety Code 11362.5 and the people who were behind the initiative. The whole experience was a positive one for all of us, and Noel had an exclusive interview for her producers.

About a week later I had to go and pick up a load from Piercy, California, as it was now ready for harvest. We left Petaluma with my three-horse trailer at around 3am and headed north on Highway 101. We arrived at about 7am and proceeded to cut stalk, invert it and stack it upright in the trailer. This trailer was about 24 feet long and in an hour it was completely full. We had put black cardboard over the already dark tinted windows, and opened the roof ventilators to relieve the moisture. When we closed the rear doors I had to trim excess leaf from around the edge of the doors with a razor knife.

We then got into my crew cab Ford 4x4 with the dogs, hooked up the 5th wheel trailer and headed south. After we passed through Willits there was a Highway Patrol checkpoint. We slowed down and got in the line up awaiting inspection. It seemed to be a sobriety/insurance/registration check. When our turn came up the officer looked right into my eyes and asked me what I had run over with my truck. It smelled like a skunk. He said, "Man that stinks, get it out of here!" So off I drove, while the boys were sweating bullets. That is just how it was back in those days, but those days would not last too much longer.

We delivered the load at our discreet location and transferred the plants into the cargo containers, hanging them upside down from wires. In the back of the container we had a dehumidifier, and in the front a large fan pushing air in. The plants were cut to length so that they would be about 18 inches off the floor and 10 inches from the ceiling. This was to allow channels for air flow and accelerate the drying process. Late at night we would completely close the sealed containers, and then re-open them at dawn. During the day the plants would become dry to the touch, and during the night they would re-wick themselves from the moisture in the stalk and branches. This process pulled all of the THC into the buds and prevented the crystals from falling off during trimming, and increased our THC yield per pound. It also tempered the smoke, and increased the natural flavor of the individual strains, leaving a pleasant trace signature upon the palate during exhale for the patient.

Through Jeremy's family in Oregon I arranged the purchase of two horses, a Tennessee walker mare and a paint gelding. The horses would provide transportation all over the property, and manure for the fertilizer we custom blended for the plants. Their cost and upkeep were minimal compared to the savings from vehicles and fertilizer. Another factor was that I was getting too old to get hurt on a dirt bike or quad-cycle. Those were for the younger members of the crew.

There was a bonus in this horse package. The mare was pregnant, and in July I would deliver a beautiful filly that I named Genesis Future Hope, or Gennie for short. It was such a satisfying experience to bring life into the world, the ranch, and our lives. This miraculous event started at around 10am, when my D.T. came in to tell me my mare was down in the corral. I went running out to her and I could see part of Gennie's head sticking out, but the mare was labored, breathing heavy and the process was stalled. I did not see Gennie's forward hooves. I kneeled down behind the mare and reached into her with my right arm and found the hoof. They were turned down and preventing the foals exit. I put my other arm in her and rolled the hooves forward as I gently pulled. I was now squatting, and by leaning back and sitting down I could slowly pull the foal from the mare. I literally had my feet up against her rump, and pulled the foal onto my lap. She was still in the sack and her eyes were closed with no movement. I was in fear of a stillbirth so I ripped open the sac by her nose and ran my hand down her muzzle from her eyes to her nostrils to clear any embryonic fluid and then closed one nostril and exhaled the biggest breath I ever took in my life into the other nostril and once again. Her eyes opened. I dragged her clear of the mare as Jeremy and the others of the crew showed up. I stood up and Jeremy cleared the rest of the sack and wiped her off. I then ushered them all out of the corral, as the mare stood up and turned her attention to the filly.

There was a bonus in this horse package, I named her Gennie

Gennie could not yet stand and it was important that she get up on her own and on her mother's tit in less than 2 hours, or she would have to be put down. A newborn horse receives all of its antibodies in the mare's initial milk during the first two hours post birth. Without this initial milk the foal will always be sickly, and eventually die.

Jeremy called our vet. I called Rhonda, and we all watched and waited anxiously as Gennie struggled to stand. We all wanted to rush in to help her, but I cautioned them not to disturb the bonding process with the mare. This was very important as her first vision was of me, not the mare.

On the fourth try Gennie was up with her legs shaking and angled out in four directions. Within 20 minutes she was taking her first steps with the nudging from Foxy, her mother. Soon she found the tit and she was nursing. The silence of the morning was now broken by cheers from the crew. I was covered with the mare's fluid from withdrawing Gennie, but I didn't care. I just sat down in a lawn chair, lit up a joint, and raised a prayer of thanksgiving to God while I waited for Rhonda to arrive.

I had such a wonderful feeling as I looked out into the corral to see Foxy and Gennie. The filly was bonded to her mother and as she walked around the corral Gennie was learning to walk, getting stronger and more stable with each step.

We were capitalizing on the vast acreage of the ranch to research various cultivation techniques. We had 10 different grow sites with 500 plants in each one. We had a recessed greenhouse, a grow and cover box, a waterfall hydro slope, a deluge slope, a row planting, a prayer garden, a "corn" field, and two other plots that my son Ryan was working on to learn the trade. We had two 3,500 gallon water tanks, a pond, and over 10,000 feet of 2 inch irrigation line and an unknown number of feet of smaller lines. The 2-inch were the main lines as our irrigation demand was around 12,000 gallons per 24-hour period, or 500 gallons per hour. Our well was at around 250 feet and was in a sweet water table that was several acres in dimension. Our neighbor was the Dutton winery and their irrigation demands were in excess of 700,000 gallons per day. We would pump the wells to fill our reservoirs at night when there was minimal demand for water. During the day most of our irrigation was gravity fed by high volume at low pressure from our reservoirs, tanks and ponds.

We used a skid loader and our tractor to mix fertilizer, 3 bales of hay, 3 buckets of dirt, 50 pounds of lime, 2 buckets of horse manure, 30 gallons of bat guano and 10 pounds of mushroom spores. We would use the tractor and skid loader against each other's buckets to push and fold the mixture, and then we would sprinkle it down with water, and cover it with a black tarp to cook it in the sun. In 72 hours we could spread it on the base of the plants. We would make this batch twice a week.

Hydroponics in an outdoor shade-house at Circle Star Ranch

In the barn we had 100 mother plants on a 20-hour light cycle that we cut clones from. The light cycle kept them from progressing out of the vegetative state, and we could produce starter plants to put into the ground 10 days from clone cutting. We had a system of continual planting, and expansion. In 12 weeks we had planted 5,000 plants that were in various stages of maturity. That would allow us to harvest in cycles. This would deter our being overwhelmed at harvest time. The system was designed so that we would harvest and trim the large buds or colas first, then we would return to pick the minor buds a few days later, allowing them sunlight that the colas had blocked. They would increase in size by 75% during those few days increasing our overall yield.

Part of the Circle Star Ranch garden a few days before the raid

What was left, the small buds would be used to make honey oil as the profit curve for trimming would decline as smaller buds are much harder to trim and time consuming. The demand for the oil was ever increasing, and I was producing it in the lab every night in a continual closed loop process that would run for six hours at a time.

I was working 20 hours a day. I would sleep for four hours and ate one good meal a day. Because of the intensive activity, and the possibility of a hostile invasion, Rhonda kept to her apartment in Petaluma - only coming out to the ranch a couple of days a week to check up on me, and make sure I was taking care of myself, and checking on the crew. She would not stay the night as only the crew was there for security reasons. We still had memories of the incident at Bond Avenue and considered females to be a hostage risk. We had designated hours for night patrol and this was done in shifts. Teams were made up of a runner and a tackler. This combination would allow us to run down a thief, and quickly be supported by another member of more weight and strength. The perpetrator would be zip tied and we would contact the local law enforcement. Bag 'em, tag 'em, send them off to jail. It worked for us, and the local law enforcement were relieved that we didn't have any firearms. Our unanimous consensus was that firearms had no place in cannabis production. They seemed to be like a contradiction in realities.

There was a lot of room to grow marijuana on the Circle Star Ranch

I really enjoyed and looked forward to the days when Rhonda would visit. We would have lunch and she would talk to the crew. Often she would take time out to talk with them individually, and personally getting to know them - expressing her deep concern for each and every one of them, and also as a group. Rhonda was always a person aware of her surroundings, and that had always provided a secure environment for the both of us. Rhonda really cared about what was going on with Genesis and the ranch, but she was perceptive enough to not openly display it. Her reservation physically allowed her to observe mentally, a trait she inherited from her father. Many times in our past it had protected us as a couple, and individually.

Now comes the part of the story that troubles me the most. It requires me to contact many from the past for their input and feelings. I must disclose an impropriety by one of my corporate officers. I am equally responsible, as I allowed it to happen in spite of my instincts, and my long term track records with members that suffered from it. Most of all I neglected to heed the warning that Rhonda had given me when she saw it coming. I can only hope and pray that writing about this and putting it into print will vindicate those who were maliciously accused, denied a defense, and scandalously discharged. To my Executive Secretary, Pam, to my computer engineer George, to my good friends and my best trimmers, ever, Don and Vicki, I profess my failure as a CEO, as the founder of Genesis, but most of all as your friend. I allowed myself to be deceived and manipulated, and in turn I lost the personnel and infrastructure of Genesis that had been created by your long dedicated hours, your hard work under extreme conditions, and most of all your loyal commitment and support.

Most of all I owe my apology to Rhonda, as she warned me that this was about to happen, was happening, and eventually carried out. She supported all of you, she personally knew you, she defended you, and I could not comprehend. I was blinded by progress and ambition, and had outgrown my humble ability to rationalize common sense. As a result, I lost the backbone of my organization. I state this here not to be forgiven (as I can understand your reluctance), but more to vindicate your reputations, and acknowledge that I was wrong, and not any of you. I took for granted a blessing that I had with all of you as my key personnel. I allowed that officer to seize control of assets without check. Funds were diverted, and a clandestine covenant was formed in alliance with a DEA agent, which led to the catastrophe at the Circle Star Ranch on September 12, 2002. It was not until my sentencing that the prosecutor confirmed the identity of the "Confidential Source of Information" which was part of the plea agreement. I cannot remove the hurt that all of you carry to this day, but I hope that my admission of the truth, and public declaration of the same, will somehow allow you to empathize with me, and understand my true remorse. In my defense I must admit that I was overworked. Genesis had blossomed beyond the capacity for any solitary individual to govern. My health was failing from lack of sleep and proper nourishment, and I was offsetting the symptoms by self-medicating with dosages of THC that were off the charts of current standards. Seeking a quick path for solutions impaired my judgment, and my foresight was replaced by retribution of hindsight. I had become short of patience and demanding. I did not listen to my subordinates. I justified all of this by focusing everyone's attention on bringing in the harvest, and promising that their needs would be met.

While I had delegated responsibilities to qualified people, and my trusted employees created a checks and balance system to maintain our integrity; I had also brought in new people with more credentials than credibility. I had no track record of them, and their merit and worth was based on their claimed achievements or scholastic accomplishments. This was not an evaluation of the condition of their heart, which only time can measure. Rather, it was an inappropriate foundation to base such a radical change in the company, and to my relationship with those I needed to hold close. In effect, I shot myself in the foot and undermined my own authority. Chaos was soon to follow, and I now had no one near I could trust. I had alienated myself from those who had followed me through good times and bad, remaining steadfast and vigilant during tribulation. Soon I would need them, but they had already been discharged with prejudice.

Genesis 1:29 sign by marijuana field at Circle Star Ranch

The DEA Raid on the Genesis 1:29 Ranch

September 12th, 2002, Sebastopol, California

In a pre-dawn raid, agents of the DEA assaulted and laid siege upon the property of Genesis 1:29 Corporation, seizing 5000+ marijuana plants, or approximately 5000 pounds of marijuana ready for harvest with an approximate street value of $27 million.

I was awakened by the feel of an AR-15 barrel pressing against my cheek below my right eye. A man dressed like a ninja in his black facemask was staring into my eyes with a cold steel glare of death, without remorse. I instinctively grabbed the muzzle of the rifle barrel and pulled it over my shoulder with my right hand, re-directing the end of the barrel past me. My left hand slapped the bolt on the top of the rifle, forcing it back as he pulled the trigger. The shell ejected and the bolt slid out of the gun as my thumb hit the button ejecting the magazine.

The rifle was now useless, and I had the terrorist in a controllable state, as the sling of the rifle was around his neck. My close proximity to him prevented his accomplice (Patrick Kelly) from shooting me, as by his own statement, "I could not get a clear shot at Schmidt without shooting James Li."

After a lengthy struggle, I was overwhelmed by more individuals and thrown to the ground, being stomped and struck with rifle butts. It was at this time that I was informed that they were DEA agents, under the command of Dan Tuey, whom I had previously been involved with in numerous confrontations in Mendocino and Humboldt County.

Some background is in order here. Our latest confrontation with Tuey was at DEA offices in San Francisco, when he was intimidating me and two other company officers to withdraw our DEA 225 forms and registration to cultivate, process, and distribute Schedule I Cannabis under the exemption provided by 21 USC 823 (a): "The Attorney General shall register an applicant to manufacture controlled substances in schedule I or II if he determines that such registration is consistent with the public interest and with United States obligations under international treaties, conventions, or protocols in effect on May 1,

1971."

The Department of Justice had issued me control numbers and I was in consistent monthly correspondence with Laura Nagel and Gloria Randall, who were the Administrative Law Judges assigned to monitor the activities and progress of Genesis.

On September 12th, the agents did not have a warrant to produce or serve, and it was not until January that this was understood by the DOJ in Washington. They did not even know of the seizure and arrest. Rather, they were annoyed that I had not responded to their recent dispatch of interrogatories. At that time they were informed of my incarceration, and they were quick to deny ever issuing a warrant for my arrest. They were in fact bewildered as to the nature of the charges and who authorized the assault.

"Meanwhile, back at the ranch..."

I was handcuffed behind my back (with a dislocated shoulder from the scuffle) and dragged by my feet, face-down out of the bedroom through the living room, out the front door, across the porch and down the stairs. My forehead struck every step. It now needed stitches. With blood in my eyes, I surveyed the situation and soon realized that all my ranch-hands, my son and his friends from college, and the rest of my crew, were all in handcuffs. At this time, I initiated the contingency plan we had created in order to deal with a scenario such as this.

In front of all the spectators, the Sheriffs, and of course the DEA, I took complete responsibility for all the activities occurring on that property at that time. This resulted in the release of more than a dozen people.

You see, the issue here is that it is cheaper for one person to go through the legal process than many.

If only one person faces the charges, then the crew cannot be manipulated. This eliminates people inadvertently saying things that can be re-construed by the investigators and used as weapons against justice. The less the enemy knows, the less they can create.

Drug enforcement agents and investigators for the prosecutor's office are not selected for their intelligence. It takes a morally bankrupt individual with below average intelligence to violate civil liberties and

166

perform unnecessary terrorist actions. They are selected for this work through psychological tests to find applicants who are eager to commit acts of violence while under the protection of their superior's orders. They are too stupid to understand that they are expendable should an investigation arise challenging the due process authority under color of law. Most of the candidates apply for these federal positions because they are not competent enough to compete in the common civilian job market. Most of the field agents are "wanna be" military soldiers that were rejected, or did not qualify for a military career (or did not have the courage to engage a real soldier in actual combat).

Most of my veteran friends laugh at them donning paramilitary outfits with weapons of war to engage in conflict with unarmed civilians. Most field operatives of the DEA do not show enough intelligence to understand that they are the laughingstock of society and other government agencies such as the Secret Service, FBI and the ATF (Alcohol, Tobacco, and Firearms). Agents such as Dan Tuey, Patrick Kelly, and James Li have become legends in their own minds. They have gotten away with armed robbery of the cash from dispensaries (that never shows up on evidence sheets), the violation of basic human rights and considerations, and the blatant lies written in criminal reports and supported by prosecutors. Law enforcement officials have become careless, and publicly declare that they are above the law, including judges and prosecuting attorneys. Their handlers (supervisors) have unleashed rabid dogs on infirm American citizens. But they have not considered that these vicious animals may turn on them when it is time to rein them in.

Our best defense is to never give (or agree to) any information that is not directly involving us, and in the event that we are confronted with an allegation, it is our duty to accept the full responsibility and burden upon ourselves as individuals. This is the tactic used by American POWs, which angered their interrogators without limit. They have nothing to work with unless we intentionally or accidentally divulge some form of information that implicates another person, thus perpetuating a domino effect.

When the DEA arrives, it's identical to the Gestapo during the rise and fall of the Third Reich during World War II. You are caught, regardless of the law and circumstances. There are no deals; there are no "do-overs" or re-plays. Our best defense is an offense, by way of damage control. It is obvious that California law is not part of the federal agenda, and we need to structure our thinking to the terms and conditions we are faced with. It is not the cards we are dealt, as much as it is how we play the hand.

We minimize the damage by way of the body count (those arrested), intelligence they can gather (documents, ledgers, patients lists, etc.) and cooperation amongst each other. Taking responsibility at the scene automatically qualifies you for a downward departure at sentencing. It also eliminates "kingpin status" if you are the only one charged. It leaves no room for negotiation, temptation, or coercion. Also, it leaves your people free, outside to help you with bond, family, legal fees, and financial support while incarcerated.

Remember this: once you cooperate with the government, they will own you for the rest of your life. Can you understand the power of blackmail? You will never, ever have peace of mind again, knowing that others may suffer as you are, because of a moment of physical, emotional, or psychological weakness. No matter what you do, you will not walk away from this, as there are other agencies that can bring charges against you, and you can never satisfy all of the wolves. Remember that your cooperation is not a secret, and your identity can be revealed by the prosecutor in exchange for the signing of a plea agreement.

What is a hero? He is the one who took the bullet for many others out of love, compassion, an unwillingness to tolerate injustice any longer. To individually take the responsibility, the strides, the consequences, so that others may live or be free. The price for this is enormous in the form of loss of freedom, pain, isolation from loved ones, and occasionally blood or worse, human life. Our parks are filled with statues of heroes, which of course become perches for pigeons and are usually covered with bird droppings. They become a place for people to meet, a landmark - but few are those who read, or even more so, understand, what that memorial represents.

We are paying a demanding price to exercise our rights guaranteed by the 10th Amendment and California law. If you consider yourself a soldier in this struggle for humanitarian privilege and basic human rights, then stand erect as a role model for those who follow, in that, by

168

our example, we all become stronger. I ask: how will you be remembered?

Incarceration 2006-2008

I was sentenced in the summer of 2005 and received 41 months. I took the offer after Rhonda and I both agreed that justice was not going to be served. I had already lost 3 years of my freedom by way of incarceration, halfway house and pre-trial status. Her health was declining, and her father had recently passed on, causing us to lose a very dear and substantial figure in our lives. I could no longer fight the good fight, and it was time to bring resolution to this miscarriage of justice. I was sentenced to the Federal Prison Camp in Lompoc, California.

Judge Breyer ordered the release of my personal property and the records seized from the offices of Genesis. I was assured that I would not be required to report until this had been completed and confirmed by my acknowledgement in court. So my first date to appear for sentencing was postponed by Judge Breyer, as the DEA had failed to cooperate with the terms of surrender. This happened again a few weeks later. Finally in September the DEA released my company records and computers. The day I picked them up at the Federal building in San Francisco I received an unexpected compliment from the agent assigned to this task. He informed me that his superiors were commenting on the accurate and extensive record keeping that Genesis had performed. Every receipt was in its original book, each of these were in numerical order in their original box. They said that they had never seen such complete chain of custody and inventory control in all their years of monitoring pharmaceutical companies and pharmacies, and commended me on the thoroughness.

Well that made me feel pretty good, as now a marijuana corporation had set a new level for quality control and accountability. Not bad for a bunch of so-called stoners. Now, where was my personal property? They could not answer that question, and recommended I call them back in a week. They would try to locate the agents who were present at the scene to find out where it was being held. The items in question were approximately 9 ounces of pure flake gold in its natural state, a Samurai sword collection with an insured value in excess of $30,000, and my lifelong collection of knives produced by the Masters of the Knife Makers Guild. These included a scrimshaw handled whaling knife by Olsen which by itself was valued at over $10,000, and many *Endino De Leon* hand forged folding knives yet un-appraised, and some Barry Wood prototypes that were numbered, signed and dated. These took the longest to collect as they only trickled in a few pieces at a time.

Evidently Dan Tuey, Patrick Kelly, and James Li did not expect these items to be returned to me and therefore split up the collection between them. It was not until Judge Charles Breyer threatened their supervisor and the prosecutor with contempt of a court order that they responded. This was finally completed by early December although a few pieces were still missing, as they were not listed on the inventory sheet. I responded to the US Marshalls for prison designation, and it was at that time I discovered that I would not be going to Lompoc, California. Instead, I was going to Leavenworth, Kansas. Rhonda and I were in shock, but there was not a thing we could do about it as the Bureau of Prisons decides where you will do your time – no matter what the sentencing judge orders. Their explanation for this was to separate me from the media, and they informed me in no uncertain terms that, "if the circus follows me," to Leavenworth that they could find a worse place to put me.

On January 6, 2006, at 4am I hugged Rhonda goodbye, gave her a long kiss, and headed for the Oakland airport for a one-way flight to Kansas City. There I would do my time without any visits, no camaraderie, surrounded by inmates who had been arrested for manufacturing methamphetamine, and crack cocaine dealers who had provided substantial assistance to prosecutors at the time of sentencing, and were doing less time than me. There were guys there who were arrested for kilograms of rock cocaine and firearms possession, who went through the Residential Drug Abuse Program before me and were on their way home in less than a year. This is just one of many examples of the power that was given to prosecutors. They have made federal judges obsolete with no more authority than a robed decoration of a day long gone by. They are symbols of the past with no more power than the American flag in the courtroom.

After 4 days short of 24 months at Leavenworth, I was released and boarded a Southwest Airlines flight to a halfway house in San Francisco. Yes, I was returning to 111 Taylor Street where I had been during my pretrial status, after 5 years of courts and incarceration. This is where I am finishing this book. I am still facing 3 more years of supervised release (probation), and as an, "enemy of the state," the Federal Government will monitor my activity for the rest of my natural life, or the end of this system of things, as we know it.

Epilogue

So I take a look back at this long strange trip that I have endured so as to put it in perspective. What have I really gained from all of this? What have I learned? Where do I go from here? Would I do it all over again? These are the questions that all of us will at some time in our lives ask ourselves. They are the basis for self evaluation that we need to measure our personal worth and our contributions to society as a whole. It is our God given conscience that propagates such contemplation. Therefore I will try to be sincere and unquestionable in my response.

History repeats itself on a regular cycle. The only changes being the players, the time and the location. The powers that be in authority at any given point in time have continually and predictably ventured into conflicts under the cloak of a humanitarian endeavor. That illusion has allowed them to proceed with the approval of their constituency to engage in brutal acts of immorality and genocide outside of their political boundaries. This is never headline news, as their governed body of citizens would not approve of this use of their revenues by either their conscience or their fear of the consequences of retaliation. Pearl Harbor and The World Trade Center are two examples of this. Wars and international conflict have never been about the welfare of human beings, they are solely about money, power, and domination. I would not have learned this fact had I not taken my life into my own hands, and embarked on this outrageous adventure that became my life. For me it is too late to turn back to that Garden of Eden where I was raised because the veil of innocence was lifted long ago. I am now spiritually motivated to encourage others to open their eyes, and take a good look around themselves - in that they may be able to make decisions based on the morality and compassion for their fellow man

I struggle daily with memories of the negative side of my adventures. Some visions will haunt me for the rest of my life. When I was encouraged to document my story, it was because of some of the humorous tales I would share among friends. These stories were always based on the comical or unbelievable situations that others and I had experienced back in the day. They were not for self-edification, but rather to encourage this new generation of activists to accept the

175

challenges of social change, no matter how ridiculous or dangerous those conditions may become. There is no way to predict the outcome of any plan that is "outside the box." The only real guarantee is that if you do not make the effort to undertake the task to improve something, there will be no change. The condition of the heart should be an essential co-efficient in the equation that formulates your plan of action.

So now I must confess that there are certain gaps in my story. To this day I am not able to talk about particular circumstances, let alone write about them, without going into a post trauma form of stress. Those people who are close to me, especially Rhonda and others like Tim Castleman, have witnessed my mental departure by my enigmatic expression and visual focus into a void on the horizon, while running my fingers through my hair, and they have not passed judgment upon me. I am grateful for that. "Nam" Veterans call them flashbacks, but I am not a veteran. So I refer to them as temporarily checking-out for a minute. There is a price for every experience in life, and I heartily encourage everyone to consider this before every decision. I can only ask this of you; that before you draw the conclusion that I was a careless adventurer in search of fame and fortune, let me clarify the fact that I always put the safety of my crew first, and brought every one of them home. I have hopes of all of us being reunited once again. We have so much to talk about, so much to share. I only wish that I could have inserted their perspectives along with mine to provide a more balanced account. If this book has entertained you, if it has moved you, then I am grateful.

Robert

CPSIA information can be obtained
at www.ICGtesting.com
Printed in the USA
LVHW111149151120
671745LV00029B/297